Mommy the ghost standing by

Ghostly Gift

Holiday Corner
Christmas Cozy Mystery
Short Read
Book #2

Ileana Muñoz-Renfroe

GHOSTLY GIFT
ILEANA MUNOZ RENFROE

Ghostly Gift

Holiday Corner Christmas Cozy Mystery Book 2

Ileana Muñoz Renfroe

Published by Ileana Muñoz Renfroe, 2022.

Copyright

DEDICATION

To my children, I love you both very much. Everything I do, I do for you. And to Eleanor, I love you.

ACKNOWLEDGEMENT

Thank you, Sharon Michaels, for including me in this very exciting 3 book series. It was great working alongside you and Donna B. McNicol to bring together such a fun project. I hope everyone enjoys reading all three books.

Thank you to my family who continue to support my dreams. A special thank you to all of my beta readers. You are amazing! To everyone in the Cozy Mystery Village and Renfroe's Reading Group, thank you for supporting my writing.

To my parents and last but not least, to my Abuela Rosa who is the inspiration behind my books.

CAST OF CHARACTERS

Edwin Bowater - Owner of Mistletoe Manor Inn. Purchased the abandoned home nearly fifteen years ago.

Thaddeus Holiday - Founder of Holiday Corner, VT 1892

Lady Louise Rafferty – Ghost. Spends her time haunting Mistletoe Manor Inn

Lord Ralph Rafferty - Lord of Parksville

Karlee - Lady Louise and Ralph Rafferty's Baby

Celeste Reed - Visiting guest. Recently having lost her husband in an accident she decides to return to Holiday Corner with her daughter to find the magic again. She is tall, with reddish hair, and green eyes

Hayley Reed – Celeste's daughter. Six years old, she often sees and speaks with her recently departed father

Recurring Characters

Joy Holiday - **Holiday Corner Events Planner** - Left for Boston twenty-five years ago, met her rich, sweet-talking husband, Calvin Bennett, divorced him, and returned to Holiday Corner to be with family.

A tall, redhead with striking green eyes, forty-five-year-old Joy has returned to her hometown. She was re-energized by the warmth and compassion of family, friends, and neighbors. The holiday spirit of their Vermont town rings true all three hundred and sixty-five days of the year.

One of Joy's favorite sayings: "What do you mean Santa Claus isn't real. Of course, he is, and lives right here in Holiday Corner, Vermont."

Nick Holiday - **Mayor of Holiday Corner** - Tall, redheaded, emerald eyed Nick is Joy's twin brother. He likes to point out how he's her much older brother by a whole ten minutes. Nick is the serious sibling, the Harvard Law School graduate.

Thaddeus Holiday, his great-great-great grandfather founded the town in 1892. Nick's job description as Mayor, is keeping the family legacy and the Holiday Corner spirit alive and thriving.

Nick has been married to Melody Holiday, his high school sweetheart, for twenty years. They have two children: Crissy is nineteen years old and enrolled in an exclusive culinary arts program in France. Gabriel, eighteen years old, is restless and can hardly wait to leave the small town to strike out on his own.

Frank (Francis) Lawson - **Sheriff of Holiday Corner** - The blonde hair, blue-eyed sheriff grew up in Holiday Corner and attended school with the Holiday twins. In fact, Nick and Frank have been best friends since they were in diapers. Tall with an athletic build, both Frank and Nick excelled in sports.

Frank's father was the sheriff before he retired. Frank was elected by a landslide to the Sheriff's position one year ago. His mother owns the local bookstore, the Corner Reads.

Frank's wife passed away five years ago and he's now raising their sixteen-year daughter Samantha on his own. He says, with a smile, "Raising a teenager is a constant test of my stamina and patience."

Frank loves Holiday Corner and is determined to serve and protect the citizens and tourists to the best of his ability.

Butch Chatwick - **Town trouble maker and owner of the local auto repair shop** - In a nutshell, Butch is a forty-five-year-old who has never grown up. In school he made it his mission to bully others before they could tease him about his weight. The "jocks" called him "stubby." No way was he going to show them how much the teasing hurt. He learned quickly, bully first before someone does it to you.

Butch has always had a chip on his chubby shoulders, especially when it comes to the Holiday family. In his opinion, the town treats the Holidays like royalty. Not him, no siree. He's made it his mission to knock them off their high and mighty pedestal.

Through high school he did everything he could to make prim and proper Joy Holiday's life as uncomfortable as possible. His goal was to make her cry. But she always had her brother or Frank Lawson somewhere nearby protecting her. Butch still vows to put her in her place. She's snubbed him one too many times. Revenge will be sweet!

Garith London - **Town gossip and all-around nosy neighbor** - Tall, boney, grey haired sixty plus year old Garith moved to Holiday Corner from London, England, ten years ago for a change of pace. Truth be told, he needed to get away from the numerous enemies he'd made as a gossip columnist for a popular London tabloid. Last he'd heard he was being sued by some big-time celebrity who wanted to get even for the slanderous story written about his wife.

Garith's philosophy is: If you can't find a juicy story to write, make one up.

To make ends meet, Garith writes under the pen name London Gray for a United States tabloid. The publication doesn't care if what he writes is true or not, as long as it is sensational, and readers buy papers.

Emily Dear - **Town's grandmother figure and problem solver** - Emily has a heart of pure gold. In her late eighties, Emily makes sure her door is always open and there's a pot of hot tea ready for anyone needing a sympathetic ear and loving hug. As a retired kindergarten teacher, Emily has known most Holiday Corner residents their entire lives.

Some people say Miss Dear has magical powers or maybe she's Mrs. Santa Claus. Emily is short and round with wire-rimmed reading glasses perched on the tip of her nose. Her silver hair is always in a sloppy bun on top of her head and her cheeks are as rosy as can be.

The cheerful smiling woman is never without her large red and green tote bag. The funny thing is, she is always able to find something in that oversized bag that seems to provide the right solution to a person's problem.

Arvin Prankish - *Holiday Times Newspaper* **owner** - Now in his seventies, Arvin still likes to liven things up in their quiet little town. He's proud to live up to the "prank" in Prankish. His blue eyes sparkle when he has the town laughing and having a good time. He'd never devise a prank that would harm anyone, but some of the past pranks have created a bit of chaos. There was that time the annual Easter egg hunt had a few freshly laid eggs mixed in with the plastic ones. Needless to say, the parents were not pleased.

PREFACE

Holiday Corner, Vermont, founded in 1892 by Thaddeus Holiday, is your typical quintessential Christmas town filled with twinkling lights, garland, wreaths, poinsettias, and red ribbons.

You're probably thinking nothing exciting ever happens in our quiet mountain town.

Let me tell you about ...

PROLOGUE

June 1908: Holiday Corner, VT

Heavy fog filled the late evening air. Lady Louise Rafferty had been staying with her husband and small child at the Thaddeus home while they were away on holiday. The Holidays had preferred to visit family during the Christmas season. So, saying at the Manor with her husband and child was the highlight of the season for Lady Louise. During this time, they did not have to worry about entertaining. Even her husband, Lord of Parksville, was able to relax and enjoy the time with his family.

As of late, there had been gatherings at the house, secretive meetings that she was not allowed to ask about but that worried her, nonetheless.

Unconventional as it may have been, Lady Louise tucked her child into bed every night together with the nursemaid. On this particular night, after she ensured her child had fallen asleep, Lady Louise Rafferty went to the sitting room to read one of her favorite books. Waiting for her husband to conclude his meeting, she had fallen asleep only to be awakened by the sound of gunfire.

Instinctively, she grabbed her shawl and opened the door. Her husband ran to her and held her tight.

"Go hide where I showed you yesterday. Do not make a sound. I will come for you as soon as we deal with this situation," he kissed her passionately.

"What is happening? What about Karlee? I can't leave without our daughter," she asked, evidence that she was terrified given away by the tone of her voice.

"Nothing to concern yourself with my darling. I'll get her and bring her to you, now hurry," he said with urgency, and ran back towards the men that had gathered in the hallway.

She overheard them talking about the grave situation and what needed to be done to prevent those outside from entering the home.

Even in the midst of the chaos, she assumed her husband would be coming for her soon, the intruders would be apprehended, and everything would go back to normal. As Lord of Parksville, she knew there were times when he had to deal with sensitive information. Maybe this time was one of those times...

Lady Louise Rafferty ran as quickly as she could to where her husband indicated she hide.

In the guest room at the far end of the room was a closet, but it was anything but ordinary. In fact it was a secret room, and behind that room there was a crawl space just big enough for her and Karlee. It had already been set up with pillows, blankets and minor essentials.

Thaddeus and his family had built this secret crawl space as a precaution not realizing Lady Louise would be the first to use the space.

Hours passed as she waited for her husband's return. She drifted in and out of sleep. Eventually, she awoke disoriented. There was no way to tell how long she'd been asleep.

Realizing her daughter had not been brought to her, she tried to open the door. Try as she might, it would not budge, it was stuck. Lady Louise screamed for her husband, begging for him or anyone else to open the door, but it was a fruitless endeavor.

Hours became days until she finally drifted to sleep in the tranquil confines of that space never to wake again.

When she next opened her eyes she felt no hunger, no thirst, no discomfort. After a while, realization set in; she was no longer in the crawl space waiting for her husband to save her. No, instead, she was once again standing in the bedroom.

Wandering the house, she noticed it was deserted. There was no sign of her husband or Karlee or anyone else for that matter. It appeared abandoned. She was completely alone.

Seasons passed and even though she continuously tried looking for her family, Lady Louise was confined to the Thaddeus home and the town of Holiday Corner. It wasn't until Edwin Bowater purchased the Manor, that she again saw people trudging about once more.

She watched as workers came and went, and still, no one could see her, not even Edwin. Time and time again Lady Louise would try to go beyond the edge of town, even if to find some quiet outside of the Manor. Regardless of what she did, every time she tried to cross over the invisible threshold, she appeared back in the room, the room with the secret crawl space.

Endless nights were spent crying and missing her family. One evening, as Lady Louise thought of her lost loved ones and wept, she began to wonder again how it was possible her life ended this way. Then, it hit her. If she was to be confined to Holiday Corner, she would haunt the town and all of its inhabitants until someone helped her find out what happened to her family.

Over the years she'd become bitter and resentful as it dawned on her that no one had taken the time to look for her, no one missed her enough to look into what had happened that dreadful night.

Where was her child, and why hadn't her husband come for her as he had promised?

PRESENT DAY

Lady Louise adjusted her dress as she heard voices downstairs. Edwin Bowater, the proprietor of Mistletoe Manor was in his office adding logs to the fireplace and discussing the upcoming holiday festivities with Nick Holiday, the mayor of Holiday Corner.

Another year, another holiday...

When were they going to learn that no matter what they do this town will forever be haunted?

Standing by the window, she tossed her hair back and closed her eyes. She could hear them talking about the tree lighting, the decorations, and the outdoor activities planned around Main Street. Taking a deep breath, she turned, faced away from the window, and moved towards the main floor. She needed a break.

Stepping outside, she looked up at Mistletoe Manor as the early morning sun shone brightly on her face. In all its interior and exterior Victorian glory, the Manor stood at the top of a hill overlooking the town.

Outside the Manor, all the windows had a single flickering battery-operated candle with a small wreath in the center. Lights were placed along the edges of the roof, and a reindeer and Santa stood outside the entranceway.

Inside, doilies were placed over tables, ornate frames covered the walls, silver serving platters were used in the dining room, and garlands of holly branches adorned the mantles and door frames as well as all of the windows throughout the Manor.

That pleased Lady Louise very much. She liked how the Manor had been restored, and on this wintry Tuesday morning, she could see frost accumulated at the base of the windows, while snow covered the sidewalks.

Christmas time in Holiday Corner had always been her favorite time of the year. She enjoyed seeing the Manor come to life as guest made ornaments, decorated the enormous tree, and participated in events. One of her favorite events was when everyone came together by the fireplace to play charades. Despite her love for Christmastime, lately, she was getting restless and somewhat bored with the repetitive nature of what her life had become.

Back inside the Manor, as Edwin and Nick were finishing up their meeting Nick remembered there was something important, he needed to tell Edwin.

"Before I forget, Joy wanted me to let you know she'll be stopping by the Manor. If not today then within the next few days to finalize activities for the gala," Nick relayed the message.

"Thank you. I'm hoping against all odds you-know-who will *not* cause too much havoc this year," Edwin responded.

"I agree. However, it seems we say the same thing every year and nothing changes," he stated appearing solemn.

"The fact that this has been happening year after year has not escaped me. Do you think this year you can finally look into the history of the Manor? Maybe you'll have better luck with your great-great-great grandfather's papers?" Edwin asked hoping he'd be able to comply with the request although it was doubtful.

"I've told you before, as far as I can remember the only other proprietor of the Manor was Thaddeus. However, to appease you I'll look into it again and let you know if I find anything new," he responded.

"Thank you. I really need to figure out a way to get rid of this nuisance. Otherwise, sooner or later the tourists will stop coming to Holiday Corner," he stated seriously.

Edwin had arrived in town a little over fifteen years prior on his way to a conference. The moment he stepped into Christmas themed town he fell in love with the location, the people, and the local mom and pop shops.

One of the things that caught his attention was the abandoned Manor at the top of the hill. Immediately he felt drawn to the house. So, without telling anyone back home of his intentions he approached the real estate office, made an offer they couldn't resist and became the new owner of Mistletoe Manor.

He was welcomed with open arms. However, there was a light hiccup to his plans. The problem wasn't the home or the town. The problem was with the unexpected guest that just wouldn't go away.

As Edwin and Nick concluded their meeting, they heard a door slam as a whiff of cold air fluttered around the room. Ignoring it Edwin opened the door to his office. As they descended the stairs, he thought to himself, *great she's here.*

From the research Edwin had done in the local library when he first arrived in town, he learned that the Manor had traditionally held a gala every season since it was first built back in 1892. Although there was never any mention in any of the articles of an uninvited guest at those events.

Without realizing what he was getting himself into, he decided the first thing he'd do once the Manor was restored was to bring back the gala, which delighted the townspeople.

Since that first year, the people of Holiday Corner looked forward to attending the annual gala. It gave them an excuse to dress up and travel back in time to an era where their only worries were which party to attend.

Now, the decorations were underway, everything was coming along nicely. In the center of the foyer stood a thirteen-foot Christmas tree awaiting trimmings. Pine swags were placed around the banisters, and wreaths hung on every door and several of the wood paneled walls throughout the Manor.

Mistletoe Manor stood four stories tall. On the main floor, was the parlor, the sitting room, and the kitchen. The second floor housed Edwin's private office and several bedrooms. The remaining bedrooms were on the third floor. On the top floor of the Manor was where you'd find the attic. It was mainly used for storage as it was extremely cold. No matter how much insulation Edwin installed in the building it always remained extremely chilly.

As Nick was leaving the Manor and saying goodbye, a few guests arrived.

"Good morning, welcome to Mistletoe Manor," Edwin said to the new arrivals.

"This place is spectacular. We couldn't believe as we drove through town that every single tree, window and available space was decorated with holiday trimmings. It's fabulous."

"Yes. It's definitely a special place and as you can imagine, we never tire of our Christmas theme," Edwin replied with a smile on his face.

"We're looking forward to spending the next week here relaxing," one of the guests echoed everyone's sentiment.

"Well, then let's get you folks checked-in," he responded.

As they completed their reservations, Edwin handed them a list of the upcoming activities in town, as well as, in the Manor, and a formal invitation to attend the gala.

"Just so that you know, if you can swing it, the gala is meant to be reminiscent of Christmases pasts, so if you wish to dress-up in costume it's great, although not a requirement," Edwin noticed everyone looking at each other and smiling.

"This is going to be the best and most relaxing vacation ever."

Edwin just smiled hoping that was true.

As Nick turned down the street he thought about Edwin's request. In reality he had no intention of looking into the history of the house. He had heard stories passed down through the family that the Manor was haunted and that the disturbances were related to a great, great someone from his past.

If this was true, he obviously wasn't going to be the one to dig up any dirt and possibly risk tainting the Holiday family's good name. He just needed to figure out a way to put Edwin off until he could think of an answer that was believable. Maybe if he distracted him with a made-up story, that would do the trick.

Lady Louise had returned and was now staring intently at Edwin as he welcomed the new guests. Standing by the front door, she had become angry again.

Why so many guests. Why do they keep returning year after year?

No matter how hard she tried everyone ignored her. That wouldn't be a deterrent though, because she had no intention of giving up on her mission to disrupt everyone's lives.

As a matter of fact, later that afternoon she would head into town. With nothing else to do, Lady Louise's sole purpose was to haunt the Manor and the townspeople of Holiday Corner.

When she was alive, her role had been as the lady of the house. She spent years taking care of her husband and then her child, overseeing the staff, and hosting parties. Life had treated her well. She had lacked nothing. The only things she cared about were her husband and child.

Looking back, she sighed thinking of their last visit to Mistletoe Manor. She recalled only small pieces, as if in a puzzle. No memory of how she ended up dead. No specifics. She didn't remember anything from her past; not even when she died.

The only certainty in her life, was that she had this uncontrollable urge to haunt, to scare, to terrorize until someone noticed her.

Having checked in the new guests Edwin turned towards the kitchen but stopped when he heard his name being called.

"Edwin!"

Emily Dear, known to everyone as the town's grandmother and problem solver, was in her late eighties. Short with wire-rimmed reading glasses, perched on her nose, Emily always had a cheerful disposition.

There was no denying she had a heart of gold. Her home was open to anyone who wanted to stop by, either for a chat or a cup of tea. She was one of those characters that you couldn't help but like. Some even said she had magical powers.

One thing was certain, she never left home without her large red and green tote bag. The most intriguing thing about that bag was the fact it *always* provided the right solution when someone needed her help.

"Emily, how very nice to see you on this beautiful winter day," Edwin smiled and moved in to give her a kiss on her cheek.

"You know I can't stay away for too long," she chuckled.

"Come on... I'm heading towards the kitchen, join me for a cup of tea?" he smiled as he ushered her towards the back, not waiting for her to answer him.

"Sure, that would be lovely. I stopped by to drop off some desserts from Chocolate Cheers and Sweet Knead. You can never have enough chocolate treats and baked goods," she said with a smile.

"Why, thank you. I was just thinking we needed to replenish our supply. You are so kind. What would our town do without you Emily Dear?" Edwin looked at Emily with a twinkle in his eyes as he rubbed his hands together and accepted the package from Emily.

Emily sat at the kitchen table and watched as Edwin handed the package to the chef telling her to make sure she didn't eat all of the pastries.

Everyone laughed knowing that was probably a useless request. Desserts from both places were known to be the best in town. People came from all over just to purchase them. Within the next couple of hours, they'd all be gone, Emily was certain of it.

"How are the decorations in town coming along?" he asked, curious to see what she thought.

"The gazebo was given a fresh coat of white paint a few days ago and will be ready to be decorated soon. As I was passing by, I noticed they were starting to put up the extra garland and red ribbons," she replied.

"That's great news. What about the huge Fraser Fir so beautifully erected next to the gazebo? Are they working on that next?" He knew this was a focal point of the town center.

"Yes, I believe so. I heard them discussing that they would start decorating the tree tomorrow. So, if you want to stop by and help... I'll be there handing out hot cider and my infamous spiked eggnog for those brave souls willing to start a little earlier than normal," she chuckled.

"Sounds like a plan," he smiled.

"Let's just hope you know who doesn't cause too much havoc and allows us to finish decorating, otherwise we won't be ready for the tree lighting ceremony," she sounded worried.

Edwin nodded in agreement knowing quite well that was a possibility.

They spoke for a while longer and then Edwin walked her out thanking her again for the wonderful treats.

After Emily departed, Edwin walked around the Inn checking to make sure everything was in place. Then, he grabbed his coat, hat, and gloves and went outside. He walked the grounds looking for any unusual disturbances. It appeared everything was quiet on this day, and that pleased Edwin.

Later that afternoon, Edwin headed into town to visit Tinsel & Toys. He had an unusual number of children staying with their families this year at the Manor, and he wanted to make sure there were enough toys. He also needed to make sure he picked up a few more supplies for the ornaments the children would be decorating.

One of the things he prided himself on was having Christmas toys for all of the children that visited the Manor.

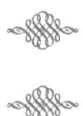

EARLY MORNING LIGHT had woken Joy Holiday, the town's event planner. Although it promised to be cold with expected flurries, Joy was ready to tackle the day.

She had just recently returned to Holiday Corner after being away for twenty-five years. In that time, she had attended school in Boston, obtained her degree in Hospitality and while working at a luxury hotel in New York City, had been swept off her feet by a charming and sweet-talking man who later became her husband.

That didn't last long though, and she found herself at forty-five, recently divorced and back in her hometown.

She embraced everything that had to do with Christmas and Holiday Corner. So much so, that one of her favorite sayings had to do with whether or not Santa Claus was real. Her answer was always the same; "Of course, he is, and he lives right here in Holiday Corner, Vermont."

Standing by her window Joy welcomed her new home with open arms. This is where she felt herself, where she had her family, and where she would begin her life again.

Joy put on her over-sized thick winter coat, woolly hat, and wrapped one of her large scarves snuggly around her neck. Smiling, she headed out the door.

The first thing she noticed when she opened her garage door was the white covered snow on her front lawn and the street surrounding her home. Realizing the snowplow had not had a chance to drive by her area, she grabbed the shovel in her garage and started to shovel just enough snow to allow her to drive out onto the street.

Her first order of business was to stop by Sweet Knead. This morning of all mornings, she needed her fix of eggnog cookies and peppermint mocha coffee. Talk around Holiday Corners was that her billionaire ex-husband, Calvin Beckett, was in town and she knew that meant only one thing, trouble.

Walking into Sweet Knead she had visions of sugarplums in her head. This was her haven, her hiding place. In fact, it was the place she went to every morning before starting the day.

Sitting with her cookie and coffee at one of the empty tables she didn't notice Garith London had entered the shop.

Everyone disliked Garith. He just brought out the worst in people. Having moved to town from London ten years prior he was the town gossip and all-around nosy neighbor.

This particular day was no exception.

"Well. Well. Who do we have here if not the famous Joy Holiday back in town? Are you following your husband?" he prodded wanting to get a rise out of her.

"Garith, always a pleasure to see you," she said through clenched teeth.

"So, I hear you're here after your husband begging him to take you back," he laughed loudly.

Everyone stopped talking and were now listening to their conversation.

"First of all, he's, my ex-husband. Secondly, he didn't leave me, I left him. So, I'd appreciate it if you stop spreading lies around town."

"You're just jealous because he's not paying any attention to you," he reiterated loudly.

The gasps amongst the other patrons were heard clearly. Everyone looked at each other and wondered if these rumors were true. To make certain that attention was focused on Garith, Joy turned the tables.

"Well, let's see, I hear you left London in a hurry because you'd made enough enemies. That you were being sued by a big-time celebrity because of the slanderous stories you wrote about his wife. If I were you, I'd be very careful what rumors you spread around here. Folks don't take kindly to lies, especially when it concerns one of their own." Then she stood and walked out slamming the door behind her.

Outside she ran into Frank.

"Wow, where're you going in such a hurry?" he asked as he stopped her from falling on the ice.

"Sorry. I went in here to have my morning coffee and cookie and behold Garith London comes in and ruins everything. That man is one of the most frustrating individuals I've ever met. I wish he'd just leave town," she spit out the words with disgust.

"Now Joy, you need to be careful what you say especially in public. It could be construed as a threat and we don't want you having to go to jail, especially for someone like Garith London," he said calmly to her.

Francis Lawson, known to his friends and family as Frank was the Sheriff of Holiday Corner.

Tall with blond hair and blue eyes, he had known Joy from childhood, having attended school together with her and her twin brother, Nick.

As a matter of fact, Frank and Nick were life-long best friends.

When Frank's father retired as sheriff Frank had applied for the position, and was elected by a landslide, at which time his father passed down the baton to his son.

His mother, still active in the community, owned the local bookstore, Corner Reads.

Frank had spent the five years since his wife had passed away, raising his sixteen-year-old daughter, Samantha.

To him, Holiday Corner was the only place on earth he could see himself living. He was determined to serve and protect the citizens and tourists to the best of his ability.

"Fine. But please try to keep him out of my way. He's spreading rumors that I'm in town following my ex-husband begging for him to take me back. What a joke!" she said as she walked away.

Frank stood on the sidewalk for a while thinking about Joy and her predicament. Her ex-husband had swooped her up once. He wondered if that was possible again?

Meanwhile Lady Louise had been removing ornaments and bows from the street lamps around Main Street, as well as, scaring some of the tourists on the sleigh rides.

Having exhausted her hauntings for now, she moved on to the local shops. First, she walked into the toy store and threw some of the toys on the floor. Then she went into the post office and threw all the mail in the air.

Where to go next?

Deciding it was time to head back to the Manor, she floated her way towards the attic.

Meanwhile, Joy had left in such a hurry she forgot to pick up pastries for her meeting with Edwin. As she looked around, she could see the townspeople gasping at the sight of the disturbances.

Smiling to herself and knowing there was nothing anyone could do to prevent them, she returned to Sweet Knead hoping Garith was no longer there.

Pleased he had departed, she went to the counter and ordered desserts and pastries to go.

While she waited for her order, she chatted with a few of the people she knew from around town.

"How are things coming along?" one of the local residents asked her.

"Everything is on target. We'll soon be announcing the date when people can start stopping by and placing their ornaments on the tree in Main Street," she replied with a smile.

"That's wonderful. Glad to hear everything is on schedule especially with what I witnessed today. Anyway, looking forward to the tree lighting ceremony. It's one of my favorite activities during the holidays," he said.

Joy was about to say something when she heard her named called.

"Sorry, got to run. My order's ready. Talk soon," she said and walked to the counter to pick up her pastries.

Once she had her goodies, she waved goodbye to everyone and headed out the door. Joy hurriedly reached the Mistletoe Manor in record time. As she walked up the steps she smiled. This place always made her feel like she was home.

The moment she entered the foyer she was enveloped in the aroma of cinnamon, holiday scented candles burning, and smoke from the crackling fire in the fireplace.

Realizing she was a little early for her meeting, she headed to the kitchen to drop off the goodies and ran right into Edwin sitting at the table drinking a cup of hot chocolate.

"Edwin. I didn't realize you'd be here. I'm a little early so I thought I'd drop these off here before our meeting," she said as she handed him the box of pastries.

"You're the second person to bring me a box from Sweet Knead today. I can tell you we never have enough, so these are definitely welcomed," he chuckled.

Placing the box on the table, he asked her if she'd like some coffee or hot chocolate.

"You know me. I can never have enough coffee."

He spoke with the cook and left instructions to bring coffee for both to the office and then ushered her upstairs.

13

Entering the office, Joy went directly to the round table. That's where they always held their meetings. And today she had brought sketches so it was easier to be able to spread everything on the table than across his desk.

They chatted a little bit and then started their meeting.

"Alright. Show me what you are thinking of doing for the gala." Edwin was excited to see what plans Joy had in mind, knowing quite well it would be great.

For the next hour they discussed the theme, the guest list, the music, the food...

"So, what'd you think? Do you like it? I've incorporated some new ideas that I think will be great for this year's celebrations," she waited anxiously for a response.

"You know I always welcome new ideas. My only concern is the same concern I have every year... will she make her presence known? Will she cause havoc and ruin the event?" he stated as he shrugged his shoulders.

"I've been thinking a lot about that and since she attends every year why not include her in the *show* so that people think we've done it on purpose?" Joy hoped he'd agree.

"Now that's an interesting concept. I definitely love your ideas and if we can include Lady Louise in the festivities maybe, just maybe, this year she'll finally realize we don't want her to leave. No! We just want her to stop the hauntings," he said as he thought of all the possible scenarios.

"Right? I mean if she's going to bother people anyway then why not make it a haunting themed gala. The waiters can dress all in white with white gloves as if they were ghosts. I can bring some dry ice which makes the appearance of smoke... you get the idea."

She was pleased that Edwin was agreeing with her vision.

"I think it's perfect. In the meantime, your brother is doing me the favor of searching through your great-great-great grandfather's papers to see if he can find anything related to our *guest*," he added.

I wouldn't count on that, she said under her breath.

"What'd you say?" He was not certain he'd heard her clearly.

"Oh, nothing I was just remembering something I have to do," she replied not making eye contact with him. She felt weird being placed in such an awkward position. Besides it wasn't her place to tell him otherwise.

"Alright, well ... I like all of your ideas and while that's a lot of work, I think you're up to the task," Edwin replied as he handed her a list of all of the activities, he had planned at the Manor leading up to the big event.

Joy read the list, smiled and nodded at several of the items. Looking up at Edwin she chuckled.

"You've also been busy Edwin," she said apparently impressed with how much he had already accomplished.

"I want this to be the very best gala Holiday Corner has ever had. Nothing's going to go wrong. I have planned everything to the very last detail," he said confidently.

Joy wasn't so sure. There was no perfect planning. She just hoped whatever happened, if anything did happen, it wasn't' too terrible.

They agreed to touch base again later in the week. The gala was the following Saturday so they didn't have much time but Joy was confident they'd be able to pull it off successfully. Edwin informed Joy he would keep her abreast of what her brother found out in his research and she agreed to let him know if anything new developed.

Joy was pleased with how everything was going and the fact that Edwin was open to her ideas. She really liked Edwin and felt bad thinking Lady Louise might dampen the mood if she tried any of her haunting during the gala. She hoped, against all odds, that did not happen. Miracles did happen in Holiday Corner. Maybe this year was *the* year.

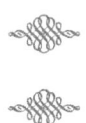

BY THE TIME LUNCH ROLLED around, Joy had confirmed several deliveries and booked the music for the gala. One of the perks of her job in Holiday Corner was that she could work from home. As she sat at her desk and looked outside, she could see children playing in the snow. That brought a smile to her face and warmed her heart. Even if her job was stressful, she loved what she was doing so much it didn't matter.

Not only was she in charge of the event at the Mistletoe Manor but had also been commissioned by the Town Council to guarantee Holiday Corner's festive holiday atmosphere. Well, that actually was a tall order! What she hadn't anticipated was the fact that lately the Santa's' they had hired to entertain the children at the gazebo on Main Street kept disappearing.

She couldn't understand who would be doing that or for what reason, but before she had a chance to investigate or contemplate the matter further, she received a call from her brother.

"Hey, did you meet with Edwin?" Nick asked.

"Yes. I was going to call you to tell you, he's hoping you look into the history of the Manor. He's convinced himself that the answers he needs to find out about the ghost can be found with our ancestors," she sounded uncertain.

"I really don't mind looking to see what I can find, but I'd rather not because if I find something that will tarnish our family name, I won't want to share that information with him. And then I'd feel guilty for not telling him the truth," he replied with concern.

"So, what're you going to do?" she asked, knowing he was in a tough situation.

"Well, now that you mention it, that's the reason I was calling you. Is there anything you can do to keep him busy and distracted? Add a new item to the list or ask him to oversee something, anything that will keep him from hounding me for answers?"

"Let me think about it, and I'll let you know if I come up with something viable," she answered not sure adding new items to the list would deter Edwin.

Back at the Manor, Edwin welcomed two new guests.

Celeste Reed had recently lost her husband in an accident leaving her to fend for herself and her daughter Hayley.

She once was a vibrant corporate executive, tall and trim with reddish hair and striking blue eyes. These days her eyes were sad, she didn't care about her appearance, and spend most nights crying herself to sleep. She felt as if she was drowning.

So, she had decided a change was needed, and the quickest solution was to get away for a change of pace. As she mulled over ideas of where to go with Hayley, Holiday Corner kept coming to mind. It was the place she had visited with her family when she was young.

Fond memories of times past kept flooding her mind. Thinking this would be the perfect getaway, she booked a room for the week, packed their suitcases and headed out of town.

Driving through Main Street, she started to feel a load had been lifted. She even slowed down so that she could show her daughter all the decorations and the small quaint shops along the way. As they approached the gazebo she told her daughter, that was where she'd go to see Santa.

Hopefully, there's a Santa this year for her to visit with Hayley, she thought to herself. Since their arrival in Holiday Corner, she seemed even more distracted than usual. Hayley, six years old, often spoke with her father. He would appear late at night to read her a bedtime story. At first, she was so excited she ran to hug him, but passed right through him, falling on the floor. She'd been confused, till he sat her down and explained to her that he was visiting and that only she could see him. He further explained that although he couldn't hold her, he still loved her dearly.

From that day on he visited her often and they would play games, or he'd read her stories. When her mother first told her they were going to Holiday Corner, she'd started crying. She didn't want to go until her father promised her, he would be home when she returned.

"Hayley, are you paying attention? We're going to spend Christmas here in Holiday Corner, a special place I'm certain you'll love," Celeste asked.

"Sorry. I was trying to speak to daddy to tell him we're going on vacation, but he's not answering me," she replied.

Going away for the holidays was Celeste's attempt to bring some joy to her daughter. As much as she tried, Hayley spoke often of her dad and how much time she spent speaking with him. That concerned Celeste. Her heart broke. How to tell her daughter that her daddy was never going to respond?

"Sweetheart, daddy is in heaven and can't speak to you right this very moment. However, he's always watching over you to make sure you're safe," she tried to be gentle.

"That's alright I was hoping to speak with him before we went on our vacation. I just hope he'll come back when we return."

Later that day, when they were officially ready to start their vacation, Celeste had forgotten all about Hayley mentioning her father. During the drive, Celeste had chatted about Santa and Christmas. She told her stories of when she was a little girl and, on those occasions, when they visited Holiday Corner. She even asked Hayley what she'd want for Christmas. The rest of the drive was done in silence until Mistletoe Manor appeared in sight.

"Look Hayley, that's where we'll be staying for the next week," she said as she pointed to the house.

"Mommy will there be other children where we're going?" She hoped.

"Yes. There's also lots of fun activities planned at the Manor. There'll be a chance for you to build a gingerbread house, paint an ornament, and even go on a sleigh ride," she told her daughter with a smile.

Hayley clapped her hands in excitement.

Pulling in to the driveway she parked the car and grabbed their suitcases.

Celeste pushed open the main door and entered the foyer. Hayley walked in behind her and abruptly stopped looking up at the staircase.

"Hayley, come here," her mother called out to her.

Hayley shrugged her shoulders and walked to stand next to her mother.

"I see we have a special guest," Edwin addressed Hayley.

She laughed as he handed her a candy cane.

"What do you say?" Celeste said.

"Thank you," she replied.

"My pleasure. Now, let's get you both checked-in to Mistletoe Manor," he responded with a smile.

Upstairs, Lady Louise had returned to the attic and stared out the window in quiet contemplation.

That child, could she really have seen me standing in the staircase? No, that's not possible. No one's been able to see me, in, well, forever.

Celeste and Hayley were given their room key, the week's schedule, and informed about the upcoming Gala.

As they settled into their room, Celeste hoped she'd not made a mistake by her hasty decision to come to Holiday Corner. A few hours later they woke from their nap, Celeste set her fears aside and decided to go into town.

"Hayley, grab your coat, hat, and gloves. I have a surprise for you," she stated.

"Where are we going?"

"I can't tell you, as I said it's a surprise," she replied and headed to the door.

Once they were downstairs, Hayley looked back at the top of the stairs. Not seeing anyone there she thought nothing of it and exited Mistletoe Manor.

Hayley skipped down the street stopping often to play with the snow. Laughing, Celeste watched her. *This had been the right decision; it would be good for both of them.*

As they approached the toy store, with a twinkle in her eye, she announced they had arrived.

"Tinsel & Toy, I present to you Miss Hayley," she laughed wholeheartedly.

Hayley giggled.

Celeste opened the door and the moment they walked into the toy store Hayley ran around cooing at everything she saw.

Lady Louise had been following them at a distance. Far up on one of the shelves, an antique doll sat looking rather dusty. The ceramic doll had rosy cheeks and blue eyes.

Hayley tilted her head to one side as she stared at the doll. Slowly, Lady Louise inched the doll closer and closer to the edge until it fell right into a basket behind the counter.

Satisfied, she moved out of the way and observed Hayley's reaction.

At this point Hayley had noticed the apparition but wasn't sure what to think. Her father when he visited appeared to be more solid. This woman was translucent. Her mother had explained there were angels all around us, this must be one of those angels she thought.

Smiling she walked up to the older gentleman standing behind the counter.

"Excuse me, I'd like that doll," she said as she pointed to the doll in the basket.

Perplexed, he crunched his eyebrows together wondering how in the world that doll, which had been on the top shelf for so many years, had suddenly fallen.

"Well, this is most unusual young lady. That doll has been in this store since before I was born. Story goes that every time they tried to bring the doll down, it somehow ended right back on the shelf. So, if this particular doll has decided to grace us with her presence, then it must mean it's meant for you," he said as he picked up the doll from the basket.

"Hayley, are you sure this is the doll you want? Look around at all of the beautiful items in the store. This doll looks like it might be an antique," she said wondering how expensive it might be, and hoping she could convince her daughter to find another toy.

"Oh, miss. Don't worry. I believe everything happens for a reason and it appears this doll wants to go home with your daughter," he said with a smile.

After he convinced Celeste, it was a gift and that she couldn't refuse such a kind offer, he wrapped up the doll in tissue paper and placed her in a box. Handing her over to Hayley, he told her to make sure she took good care of it.

"I promise to always take care of her, thank you," she said with a grin.

"Do you want to stop and get something to eat in town or would you prefer to head back to the Manor?" Celeste asked.

"Let's go back to the Manor. I want to play with my doll," she said looking from her mother back to her doll.

Celeste smiled, wrapped her arms around her, and kissed her several times. Giggling Hayley kissed her back. When they arrived at the Manor, Hayley went straight for the sitting room. The fireplace was crackling and there were several small children near her age sitting close by playing a game.

Celeste looked around the room and felt warm inside. This was exactly what she had hoped would happen once they arrived at Mistletoe Manor.

She searched for Edwin and when she found him, she asked if it was alright to leave Hayley downstairs while she went to her room to retrieve a book.

"Of course. You see over there; that young lady supervises the room and oversees the children when they're in here. They already know they can't leave unless they speak with her first. Let's make sure Hayley knows the rules," he said as he walked her back into the sitting room.

"Hayley, how are you doing? I see you've purchased a new doll?" he asked.

"Yes, my mommy bought this for me. Isn't she beautiful?" she beamed.

"She's gorgeous. Well, I just wanted to stop by and tell you that you can stay here as long as you want. However, if you want to go back to your room or anywhere else in the Manor you must first speak with that lady standing there in corner with the red apron. She's in charge here if for any reason your mother is not in the room," he said as he pointed to the corner.

"Alright," she replied.

"Thank you, Hayley, now let's meet some of the children," he ushered her towards the group sitting on the floor.

"That's alright. I just want to play with my doll," she replied as she looked up at Edwin.

Looking at Celeste he nodded and addressing her, told her if she needed anything to let him know.

"Honey, I'm just going to go upstairs to our room to get a book so I can join you. You heard what Mr. Bowater just told you right? You can't leave this room until I return or unless you tell the nice lady in the corner," she repeated.

"Yes. I promise," she replied and went back to talking to her doll.

Satisfied, Celeste left Hayley in the sitting room while she went upstairs for her book.

LADY LOUISE HAD BEEN watching the exchange and for once in her life felt hope as she watched the little girl, they called Hayley playing with that doll.

That doll, she could have sworn she'd seen it somewhere before. Her memory was not what it used to be, and she had trouble remembering anything from the past.

She slowly approached Hayley, sat on an empty wing chair in front of where she was playing, and as she observed the scene before her, smiled. This little girl reminded her of her daughter.

Oh, how I wish my Karlee was here. I miss her so.

Hayley looked up and noticed she had her hands covering her eyes.

"Don't be sad," she said looking directly at her.

Suddenly, Lady Louise looked shocked.

Looking around the room she wondered if she was actually speaking with her. Could it be possible? No!

With trepidation she looked at Haley and asked, "Can you actually see me?"

Haley stared at her for a while before responding thinking that was an odd question.

"Well, yes ma'am. I can see you. Can you see me?" she asked in return uncertain why she was being asked the obvious.

What a delightful child.

"You see, I have been stuck in this Manor for as long as I can remember and you my darling child are the only one that has seen me in all that time." Warmth filled her heart.

"I miss my family; my husband and baby," she continued in a sad tone. "Do you think maybe you could help me find my family?"

"I'll have to ask my mommy," Hayley replied staring at the apparition.

Lady Louise nodded. She was so grateful someone had finally been able to see her and speak with her, that waiting until Haley spoke with her mother would be fine.

Hope, there was hope again, that maybe, just maybe she'd be reunited with her family.

She watched Haley as she continued to play with her doll. Then it dawned on her that it was one of the dolls she had brought with her to Mistletoe Manor so many years ago.

This was the doll she had placed in her baby's room.

"Hayley, I believe this doll belonged to my daughter. I'm so glad you found it. Where did you actually find it?" she asked knowing the answer.

"In the toy store. It fell off the top shelf and the man behind the counter said it was meant to be so he gave me the doll."

Just then Celeste had returned and watched as Hayley talked to herself. She would need to speak with her when they returned home about all of these imaginary friends. Speaking with her dad and saying they were having a conversation often was not good for her.

As she approached, Hayley looked up and smiled.

"Mommy, can I help this nice lady find her family?" she asked as she looked at Lady Louise.

Celeste looked around before answering, confirming there was no one there.

"Of course. I'm sure that would make the nice lady very happy. Does she have a name?"

Not certain of the answer she shrugged her shoulders and looked up.

"I'm sorry. Let me introduce myself. I'm Lady Louise Lafferty," she said as she bowed.

Giggling, Hayley repeated her name.

"Well, that's a very interesting name. How on earth did you come up with such a long name?" Celeste asked intrigued by her daughter's imagination.

Hayley confused, looked first at her mother then at Lady Louise and back at her mother.

"I don't understand the question mommy," she replied looking back and forth between them both.

"Sweetheart, that is not a common name. Have you heard that name before?"

"No. She told me her name," she answered as she pointed at the apparition. "Can't you see her?" she asked.

"No honey, there is no one standing there. All I see is the fireplace. You know we may have to talk about this when we get home. First your father, and now this?"

"It's alright Hayley, your mother cannot see me. The fact that you can is such a relief, we'll just have to convince your mother I am standing right next to her," Lady Louise said.

"Alright. Can I go back to playing with my doll?" she asked.

In unison Lady Louise and Celeste said yes.

Hayley looked at both and giggled.

"Thank you," she replied

Just as she was about to go back to playing with her doll, one of the children approached her and asked if they could play together. Nodding, they walked over to where the others were gathered and Hayley was introduced to the group. Celeste could hear they were talking about painting ornaments to put on the tree in Main Street.

Satisfied all this talk about helping a ghost was short lived, Celeste opened her book and settled in to read. She smiled as she watched Hayley enjoying herself with her new friends.

Lady Louise retired to the attic, so many thoughts going through her mind.

For the first time in a very long time, she remembered the doll. It was indeed the doll she had brought for Karlee. That last night, she had placed it in the closet to give to her the following day.

Slowly she was beginning to remember. Finally, there was hope.

The rest of the afternoon was quiet. For the first time in years, there were no disturbances, no banging of doors, no whiff of cold air, and no scary ghost.

GHOSTLY GIFT

"GET ME ALL OF THE INFORMATION we have on Mistletoe Manor and Thaddeus. It's time we did a story on the history on the Manor and the founding father of Holiday Corner. We'll add footage from the past events and include this year's event. Especially since it promises to be one of the best galas of the century," Arvin Prankish said to his assistant.

Arvin now in his seventies is the owner of Holiday Times Newspaper, the one and only paper in Holiday Corner. Known for his pranks, he enjoyed livening things up whenever possible. Although one good thing about Arvin was that he had never devised a prank where someone had been hurt. His pranks were always harmless.

"Sure thing. There isn't a lot of information, most of what we have has been archived. There is one place I haven't looked."

"Where?" Arvin asked.

"The library. I know there is a section that is not known to most people about events that occurred during the time that Thaddeus lived in Holiday Corner. Maybe there is something there that can help us write a "killer" story."

"I love the idea. Yes, please go to the library and gather as much information as possible and let me know when you have everything. We can then decide what information can will be included."

The assistant started to head out when Arvin remembered something else.

"By the way, see if you find anything about the ghost that haunts Mistletoe Manor. That ghost must have been alive sometime in the past, which in turns means something must have happened in that Manor. I know Nick wouldn't like to bring shame to the family name, but maybe it was an accident or even if it were murder, it's time we found out what really happened and who this ghost is that seems intent on scaring our guests and our townspeople."

"I'm glad you mentioned that because I was thinking about looking into this so-called ghost to see if I could find anything and then just present you with my findings. Now that I have carte blanche I can comfortably search the records, maybe even interview a few folks who might remember or know something about the ghost."

"Let's keep this to ourselves for now. Try not to conduct any interviews unless I give you the okay. We don't want Nick or Joy upset, or trying to thwart our efforts," Arvin told her.

Satisfied with the assignment, Arvin's assistant went off in search of answers. Arvin while he sat in his chair and thought about what it might mean if there actually had been a murder in Mistletoe Manor so many years ago. And, if so, was Thaddeus or one of his descendants responsible for the crime?

Regardless, being known for his pranks, he went about devising a plan which he would implement during the gala. You can't have a modern-day event such as this with a ghost in residence and not have a prank. He laughed as the wheels in his mind started to turn.

A few hours later Arvin's assistant returned with a stack of documents and a few books.

"Boy, it seems you found information for me?" Arvin chuckled.

"Yes, and you won't believe what I found," she said with a smile.

"Do tell." Arvin was now excited to see what had been unearthed.

"Not yet. Let me put everything in order and provide you with a summary before I present to you what I found. All I can say is that you'll be pleased and possibly shocked."

She'd already begun organizing the material she had found.

"Alright. I'll leave you to your research. Let me know if you need any help. In the meantime, I'm going to head out. It's late already and I need to finish buying Christmas gifts. If I don't do it now, I'll never find the time. If you need me, I'll be at the Dash-In with Frank, Nick, and Edwin," Arvin said.

"Have fun shopping."

"Funny. You know how much I hate shopping. At least I'm meeting up with my buddies and that will make up for this torturous activity," Arvin laughed as he gathered his coat, scarf, and gloves.

Closing the door behind him, he looked around to see the streets were filled with tourists and locals alike. Children played in the snow and the adults stood by drinking what appeared to be hot chocolate. *Perfect.* He thought to himself.

This time of year, there were more decorations than usual; twinkling lights, red ribbons on wreaths, and garlands. Although Holiday Corner was decorated year-round as if it was Christmas time, during the month of December there was something special about it that made everyone smile and be cheerful which made this town most magical.

He wondered what surprise his assistant had found. Could it be the answer to who was the town's ghost? Could there have been a murder committed at Mistletoe Manor?

The more the pondered the thought, the more excited he became to see what stories awaited him. He could feel it in his bones. This year was definitely going to be memorable.

At the same time, Edwin headed out of the Manor towards the center of town to meet up with Frank, Arvin, and Nick.

As he walked the streets of Holiday Corner, he noticed the first evening stars and the white twinkle lights from the windows and doorways along Main Street. He saw the streets filled with tourists. In the park, the sleigh rides were filled with giggling children and smiling parents. He too marveled at everything that was Holiday Corner.

One thing, this year, it seemed there were more tourists than usual. That pleased Edwin, as he had grown to love Holiday Corner. It was his home and he cared about preserving its history.

Sometimes it felt as if he had lived there all his life, as if the town had purposely drawn him there. Regardless, he knew this town was where he belonged.

Edwin pushed the door open to Dash-In as a jingle-bell song greeted him. The store, like the window, was decorated for Christmas. There was a tree in the corner covered in layers of lights and ornaments, door frames covered with garland, and shelves had white fleece lining them, making it seem as if it was freshly fallen snow. There was even a snow globe on the counter near the entrance where children sometimes stopped by to give it a shake.

The proprietor played Christmas music throughout the year and folks didn't seem to tire of the repetitiveness of it all. It was said that whenever a child shook the globe and made a wish, Santa would bring them an extra secret gift on Christmas Day. Of course, that was no secret, and someone at the diner kept tabs on the children that shook the globe. But it was all in good fun and no one ever revealed the "secret" of the snow globe.

"We're over here," Nick said to Edwin as he looked around the diner.

Nodding he closed the door and headed to the corner table. Already seated were Arvin Prankish from the Holiday Times, Nick Holiday, and Frances "Frank" Lawson the town's sheriff.

"Gentlemen, good evening," Edwin said as he sat down.

They each greeted him in return.

"How are the new arrivals settling in at the Manor?" Nick asked.

"Everyone seems to be pleased with the food and the activities. Don't expect any complaints. Well, unless it's about the usual noise and the draft," he rolled his eyes.

"There must be something that can be done?" Frank asked.

"I have tried, but can't find anything related to the ghost," Edwin replied.

For a split second, Nick looked down as he avoided eye contact with Edwin. Only Arvin noticed. He needed to mention this to his assistant in case it related to the information gathered from the library.

Then as if nothing had happened Nick spoke.

"Oh, before I forget. I'm sorry my friend but I couldn't find anything in the books or papers about a ghost haunting the house. I tried but no luck," Nick made an effort to sound sincere.

He did feel awful lying to Edwin about searching for some mention of a ghost. He just couldn't afford to find anything that would in turn tarnish the good name of Holiday. Besides, he was certain there had never been a murder or any such thing happen in his beloved town. That is something he would have definitely heard about from one of his family members.

"Thank you, Nick. I can't tell you how grateful I am you at least tried," Edwin replied.

"No problem, my pleasure," Nick said feeling rather guilty at telling his friend a lie.

"Well, if you two are done I'd like to get this meeting started. I still have a few Christmas gifts I need to purchase and would like to get to the stores before they close," Arvin said.

The waitress stopped by to take their orders before they could start their meeting. Once she was gone Frank spoke.

"So, how are the preparations for the gala coming along?" he asked Edwin.

"Everything is going according to plan. Joy did bring up a brilliant idea. Make this year's event a themed one. We will be focusing on our resident ghost and making things spooky but fun, a mystery of sorts. I just hope that doesn't offend anyone," he replied.

"In the past everyone has dressed up in Victorian attire. Are you planning the same this time?" Arvin asked.

"I left the theme up to Joy to decide. She had some great ideas when we met. I'm certain she'll make an announcement in plenty of time for everyone to decide if they want to participate. You know that the attire is always optional so that shouldn't deter anyone from attending. All I know is our focus this year is to make this the most memorable gala in all of Holiday Corner history," Edwin said smiling knowing he had said the same thing earlier.

Nick was not certain that would be a good idea but kept his thoughts to himself. If the ghost that resides in Mistletoe Manor had been murdered, she may not be too keen to have a themed party that focuses on her, especially since no one knew who *she* was.

"Sounds good. Well, let me give you all an update on what's been happening around town. As you know there are several Santas, that were hired that have gone missing. We still don't know why or how, but I have everyone keeping their eyes open," he informed the group.

"That's never happened in the past. I wonder why now?" Nick asked sounding concerned.

"Weird. Maybe we can do a short story in the front page about what is happening and see if anyone has any leads. I hadn't written anything as to not alarm the townspeople. What do you all think?" Arvin asked.

"It's unusual for you to ask our opinion," Nick stated.

"True. This time though, I'm not sure of the best course of action," Arvin replied.

"I don't have a problem with you printing anything related to this incident. It isn't as if the townspeople aren't already talking about it," Frank replied.

"Good. That's what I thought. I'll make sure to have something included in the next issue," Arvin replied.

"From my end, I also wanted to let you all know that our town's trouble maker is at it again. He's been harassing the tourists and generally causing havoc around town," he stated.

"Do you think it'll get out of hand?" Nick inquired.

"No. It's harmless, just annoying," he answered.

"Anything else?" Nick asked.

"Yes. Garith. He just doesn't know when to quit. Recently he's been bothering Joy. He's been spreading rumors around town that she returned to Holiday Corner to beg her ex-husband to take her back. She was not very happy and has told him so. But knowing him, he'll ignore her and continue his gossiping."

"Well, if I hear him saying anything anywhere near the Manor, I'll be certain to put a stop to it," Edwin replied.

They talked about the upcoming big event and each gave their updates on what was happening in their end of Holiday Corner. When they concluded their meeting, they parted ways promising to keep an eye out for any unusual incidents around town.

THE NEXT MORNING, LADY Louise was back at it again. Tormenting the tourists in town was the highlight of the morning gossip. Everyone that was in town for the first time was whispering about the unusual disturbances. The locals on the other hand were not contributing to the gossip, hoping the ghost would leave them alone long enough for them to enjoy the festivities.

Deciding she'd done her deed for the day and hoping that Hayley would still be willing to help her, Lady Louise headed back to Mistletoe Manor.

The Manor was bustling with guests. Breakfast was being served in the main dining room with a separate table for the children. They were giggling as they were presented with their pancakes decorated to look like Santa's face. Edwin's purpose strove to make their experience as much fun as possible in hopes they'd return year after year.

Lady Louise was just floating into the Manor when Hayley and her mother were walking down the stairs. Hayley smiled and waved. Her mother looked around trying to see who it was she was waving to, and not seeing anyone in particular, asked her.

"Hayley, who are you waving at?"

"Mommy, the ghost standing by the door of course," she looked at her mother with a smile.

"Of course," Celeste not certain how to address the matter.

"Can't you see her?" Hayley asked rather confused.

"No sweetheart. I cannot see her. Can you describe her to me?" she asked.

"Yes, mommy. She tall," she replied.

"That's all?" Celeste asked.

Not certain how to answer she looked at Lady Louise. Smiling she told her what to say.

"She is wearing a long skirt and a white cotton shirt. Her brownish hair is up in a bun. Oh, and she's very sad," she told her mother.

"Wow. That's very descriptive and you say she's sad. How do you know that?" she asked.

"Because she told me what to say. The sad part I can tell by looking at her eyes," she replied.

At that moment Lady Louise placed her hand over her chest and sighed. This was the person that was going to help her find her remains and hopefully her daughter. Of that she was certain.

"Can you tell me more about her?" Celeste asked.

"That's the problem. She' can't remember. All she knows is that she can't leave Holiday Corner. She's stuck here and she needs our help to find out what really happened to her. Oh, and she wants us to help find her daughter," Hayley said.

"Her daughter? Her daughter is missing?" Celeste asked.

"Yes. She says this doll belonged to her daughter. She's the one that knocked if off the shelf when we were in the toy store," Hayley replied.

"Well, do you think she would answer some of my questions?" Celeste asked looking around the foyer.

Hayley looked at Lady Louise and shrugged waiting for her to answer the question.

Lady Louise looked directly at Celeste and spoke.

If you promise to help, find out what happened to me and where my daughter is now, I will answer all of your questions.

Celeste stood there waiting not having heard a word.

"She says, yes she'll answer all of your questions as long as you find out what happened to her and her daughter," Hayley repeated.

"Alright. For now, we have to go in and have our breakfast. We will start investigating later today if that's alright with," Celeste didn't finish the question as she didn't know the name of the ghost.

"Excuse me. What is your name?" Hayley asked the ghost.

"I'm sorry for being so rude. I should have introduced myself from the beginning. My name is Lady Louise Rafferty. I'm pleased to formally meet you," she said.

Hayley giggled.

"Want to share what's so funny," Celeste inquired.

"She's funny," Hayley replied.

"So, does she have a name?" Celeste asked again looking around the foyer.

"Sorry. Yes, her name is Lady Louise Rafferty," Hayley replied.

"Well, Lady Louise Rafferty. It is a pleasure to meet you. As I said just a moment ago, once we finish breakfast, we'll head over to the library to gather as much information as we can about the haunting of Mistletoe Manor," Celeste stated.

Thank you so very much. No one has been able to see or hear me in, well, forever. I look forward to seeing what you uncover. By the way, please call me Lady Louise. Although, Lad Louise knew Celeste would not be able to hear anything she said.

Hayley smiled as Celeste walked towards where breakfast was being served. She waved at Lady Louise who in turn waved back.

Celeste didn't really believe her daughter was speaking with a ghost but she figured she would indulge her for now and later today would sit her down and tell her she needed to stop this nonsense. The last thing she wanted was for her daughter to be ridiculed for talking to a ghost.

Lady Louise watched them walk away and was somewhat wary about Celeste's promise. She wondered if she was sincere in wanting to help uncover what had happened all those years ago in Mistletoe Manor. Or, was she just saying that to appease Hayley? Only time would tell. Once thing was certain. If Celeste was not telling the truth, she would bring down such a wrath, the likes of which had never been seen in Holiday Corner. No one took Lady Louise for a fool.

As they sat down to breakfast, Celeste kept running the conversation she'd just had with Hayley over and over again in her mind.

Could her daughter really see the resident ghost? In fact, if that were true, was she really conversing with her father as she had mentioned?

She abandoned her thoughts of the ghost as they were presented with the Manor's famous pancakes. Hayley giggled.

"Mommy, look. My pancakes look like Santa," she was grinning from ear to ear as she pointed to her plate.

Celeste laughed as she too was given a plate decorated with images of Santa.

"How much fun. I don't remember them doing this in the past," she said.

"This is something new we started doing several years ago and it's taken off to the point that people come just for the pancakes. One time, we decided to see what happened if we stopped decorating the pancakes and we had so many complaints we brought it back on the menu and well, here we are," the waitress said with a smile.

"Well, I'm glad, this is genius. I love the idea and most importantly the pancakes taste amazing," she said as she tried her first bite.

"Enjoy. And, if there's anything else you need. Let me know," the waitress said as she walked to the next table to take their order.

The rest of breakfast they ate in silence. When they were almost finished, Celeste asked Hayley if she wanted to go on a carriage ride. Excited she clapped her hands in response. They headed up to their room to gather their coats, gloves, and hats and headed out.

Lady Louise watched at a distance wondering if they were going to the library. When she realized they had stopped at the carriage rides, she returned to the Manor. Not certain yet if she could trust Celeste, she decided to wait until later in the evening before she made a final decision.

BY THE TIME CELESTE and Haley finished playing in the snow, participating in the children's activities on Main Street, and the carriage ride they were ready for lunch.

Thinking it might be fun for Hayley, Celeste decided to have lunch at the Dash-In. The diner was bustling with customers. The first thing that Hayley noticed when she walked in was the snow globe.

"Look how pretty," she said pointing.

"It's not nice to point Hayley. Although you are absolutely correct. It is beautiful," she answered.

As they were being ushered to their table, they were told that Hayley could go back to the counter and shake the globe, but only if she made a wish. Looking at her mother she waited in anticipation. Then not being able to contain herself any longer asked.

"Can I please go make a wish?"

Laughing, her mother encouraged her to follow the waitress to the counter. She could see when Hayley picked up the globe, closed her eyes tightly and shook it. She wondered what her wish would be.

Hayley returned to the table and they placed their order. When she was distracted, the waitress returned and told Celeste that they always inform the parents the wish of the children. Closing her eyes and sighing, she told her that Hayley's wish was for her father to come visit her at the Manor and meet the ghost.

Celeste looked at her rather oddly and thanked her. She wondered.

Could Hayley really have the ability to see ghosts? Has she really been talking with her father? All of these she had already pondered before but now she was starting to think there was some truth to all of these ghostly activities.

Word around town was that Emily Dear might know something about this so-called ghost. After lunch she would sign Hayley up for an activity at the Manor. She'd then headed out to the library to do a little research. If she was going to believe a ghost needed her daughter's help, then she needed to be prepared with as much information as possible.

During this time, Lady Louise was watching them and had heard Hayley making her wish. That was a good sign, and when Celeste reacted to hearing about her daughter's wish, she decided to give her a little nudge by causing a draft. Although she wasn't necessarily aware that it was happening on purpose, she at least wanted to make sure that, yes, a ghost existed.

When the waitress stopped by with the check, Celeste took the opportunity to ask her.

"I have a question and you may find it rather odd. However, earlier when we were talking, I felt a draft, but as I looked around the diner no one else seemed to react to it. Was I imagining it?" she asked.

"Oh no, that's the ghost of Mistletoe Manor. I'm certain she was bothering you on purpose. She tends to frighten the tourists quite often. So, if all you felt was a draft take that as a good sign. Who knows, maybe she likes you," she replied smiling.

"So, everyone in this town believes in the ghost that haunts Holiday Corner?" she asked.

"Yes, of course. Why would we not?"

Celeste shrugged not wanting to tell her she thought everyone was a bit off their rocker. Thanking her for a wonderful meal, she and Hayley bundled up and left the diner.

On the way back, she asked Hayley if she'd like to participate in one of the activities at the Manor. Of course, she jumped at the offer. When they arrived, Celeste went to inquire about available options. Finding the one she knew Hayley would like, she signed her up and told her she'd be working on Christmas puzzles and having a tea party.

Hayley was so excited she jumped up and down.

"Thank you," she said all excited.

"You are most welcome. By the way, I have to go run an errand while you're at your activity. Will you promise to stay with the other children and not wander off anywhere?" she asked.

"Yes," she replied

Looking behind Celeste she nodded and turned around to look at her mother.

"Lady Louise said she'll watch over me," she said with a smile.

Celeste turned around hoping she'd see even a shimmer. Turning back to face Hayley, she told her she was grateful someone was watching over her.

"She says thank you."

"Tell her thank *you*," Celeste looked around the room and smiled.

They went upstairs to put their things away. Hayley put her doll on the bed and told her mother that she would be taking a nap. Celeste felt so much happiness at that moment it melted her heart.

While Hayley was singing to her doll, Celeste sat on the bed and made notes about what she wanted to find out; when the Manor built, if there were any mention of the ghost in any of the documents at the library. She even made a note that if she had enough time she'd stop by the local newspaper. Maybe they had stories about the ghost.

When she was done, she told Hayley she was ready to go downstairs.

"We don't want to be late for your activity," she said.

"I'm ready. My doll has gone to sleep and Lady Louise is ready to watch over me," she said as she walked to the door.

Celeste had never thought the ghost would be in the room with them. She wasn't certain that was something she was comfortable with, but for now she remained silent.

After dropping Hayley off in the activity room, she headed out to the library. The walk was just what she needed to help gather her thoughts.

When she arrived, she inquired as to where she could find the history of the town and Mistletoe Manor. She didn't mention anything about the ghost as she didn't want the librarian to think she was crazy.

Once she was in the correct section, she began pulling out books and gathered as much information as she could find. At the table, she spread everything out in chronological order. Sitting down to sort through the documents she lost track of time quickly. Realizing how much time had passed, she gathered everything and returned it to its proper place.

Leaving the library, she thanked the librarian.

"I hope you found everything you were looking for?" she asked.

"Somewhat. Actually, I was wondering if there was anyone in town who would have first-hand information on the history?" she said mostly to herself.

"Well, now that you mention it, you might want to speak to Emily Dear. She's been in Holiday Corner for as long as I can remember. Not sure if she can help, but worth the try."

"Oh, thank you. I'll reach out to her. One last question, do you know where I can find her?" Celeste asked.

Chuckling, she answered.

"Where can you not find her. Emily is always around. You won't be able to miss her. I believe for the next few days she'll be on Main Street serving her specialties to the workers. If not just ask any of the locals, they'll direct you to Emily," she replied.

"Thank you," Celeste said as she headed out the door.

"Enjoy your stay in Holiday Corner and I hope you find what you're looking for."

As Celeste headed back to the Manor, she felt much better about her plan. Something told her Emily Dear would be a big help.

CELESTE SAT AT THE Daily Grind, the local coffee shop, drinking a peppermint coffee and nibbling on a chocolate chip muffin while she waited for Emily. The previous night when she was in the library at the Manor, Edwin had walked in and they'd spoken briefly about her desire to learn the history of the town and Manor. He too had suggested she meet Emily Dear. And so, just like that, he'd called Emily and asked her to meet Celeste the next morning for coffee.

As if on cue, the bell over the door rang, indicating someone's arrival. Emily walked through the door and greeted everyone and then strolled over to where Celeste was sitting.

"Hello my dear. The perfect place to meet on a cold day like today. Let me place my order and I'll be right back," she stated as she headed to the counter.

Once finished placing her order, she returned to the table and sat down.

"Edwin told me you were interested in learning the history of the town and Mistletoe Manor. I would be delighted to provide you with any details I may know, although I'm not certain there's much I can offer," she said.

"First of all, I wanted to thank you for meeting me. I understand this time of year you are extremely busy. That being said, I did some research in the library, but didn't find what I was looking for," she said warmly.

"You mean to tell me there's no information in the library about Holiday Corner or even Mistletoe Manor?" she gasped as she asked the question.

"No, no. Sorry. I think I need to be honest with you," she said almost in a whisper.

Emily's eyebrows were raised as she wondered what could be so secretive that she needed to whisper.

"Well, you see, it started when my daughter Hayley started talking to what I thought was an imaginary friend. However, it turns out she says it's not an imaginary friend at all but the ghost that haunts the town, and of course, the Manor," she said looking down rather embarrassed to even be talking about a ghost.

Emily laughed before she continued.

"I'm sorry. I don't mean to make light of what you are saying it's just that everyone in town knows about the ghost. It's not a secret. Actually, there are some that have said they seen a glimmer of something or other. However, no one has actually seen the ghost," she replied.

"That's the thing. My daughter says she can clearly see the ghost and even knows her name."

"What? She actually knows her name? Now that's something no one has been able to find out. I believe as much as they have searched there's no mention anywhere how this ghost came to be," Emily said.

"Hayley introduced me to her even though I couldn't see her. Her name is Lady Louise. The problem is she apparently can't remember what happened to her or how she came to be in Mistletoe Manor and that's what she was hoping Hayley could help her with. I'm concerned that a ghost is speaking to my daughter. So, I thought if I looked into the story, I might be able to find out more about why she's here, and why she hasn't not moved on," she said.

"Very interesting, very interesting indeed," Emily said as she thought about what Celeste had just told her.

They stopped talking when their orders arrived so that they could enjoy some of their breakfast before continuing.

"I don't know that I can be of much help but ask away. If I can answer any of your questions, I'd be more than glad to. As a matter of fact, if you don't mind, I'd love to investigate this along with you and Hayley," she said hopeful Celeste would agree to let her tag along.

"Of course. That would be wonderful. I'm still a little hesitant about believing a ghost is speaking with my daughter, but too many little things have happened since we've arrived in Holiday Corner to dismiss my daughter's wish to help the ghost find her daughter," Celeste stated.

"Her daughter?" Emily asked.

"Yes, apparently the reason Lady Louise has not moved on is because she can't find her daughter," she replied.

"From what I remember, my parents mentioned at one time something about a missing woman. It's been so long I can't recall exactly the conversation, just that it had something to do with an affair, sorry. Although several years back, I did do some research on Thaddeus Holiday. I didn't learn much except that he founded this town and built the huge Manor where you're staying."

She took a bite of her muffin and Celeste waited patiently for her to continue her story.

"Not many know this, but there are a few who believe Thaddeus was having an affair with a woman who would visit the house during the summers. From what I have heard, one day she left with her daughter to never return. Although I have never believed this story as there's no proof," she stated.

"I'm wondering if this is the same person that's been haunting the Manor? Whether or not they had an affair, do you happen to know what happened to her? Can you tell me anything about her and her daughter?"

Laughing and with a twinkle in her eye Emily smiled.

"Breathe," she patted Celeste's hand as she continued.

"As I said, those are only rumors. There has never been any indication that Thaddeus cheated on his wife. There has to be another explanation as to the ghost haunting Mistletoe Manor," she said.

The waitress interrupted them again, this time to ask if they wanted anything else and overheard them talking about the ghost.

"Are you interested in finding out who our resident ghost?" she asked excitedly.

"Well, maybe. Yes actually. Can you tell me anything about her?" Celeste asked.

"Her? You mean to tell me you know it's a woman?" she said her eyes bulging.

"I believe her name is Lady Louise. Have you ever heard any mention of her by name?" Celeste asked.

"No. Only that Holiday Corner has a ghost, a very active ghost," the waitress replied.

Celeste and Emily waited until she left before continuing their conversation.

"Is there anything else you can think of that might help me with my research?" Celeste asked.

"There are some books in a locked room in the library that are not available to just anyone that might shed some light into your investigation. However, there are only two people that have a key to that room. One, is Nick Holiday and the other is me," she giggled.

"You? You have a key?" Celeste was shocked at this revelation.

"Yes, I have a key to the library. Nick entrusted me with it a long time ago," she smiled.

"Do you think I could have access to the documents?" Celeste asked in anticipation.

"Yes, of course my dear. Let's plan on meeting tomorrow after hours at the library. Not many people know about the locked room and I don't want any nosy locals snooping around and discovering our secret," Emily's eyes twinkled.

THE NEXT MORNING CELESTE woke up unsure if investigating the history of a ghost that no one else in town had done anything about was such a good idea. Hayley had been playing with her doll and talking to someone she assumed had been Lady Louise.

There was no denying that the ghost existed especially when she was around because the temperature dropped significantly.

"Lady Louise, if you're here may I ask you some questions?" Celeste felt silly as if she were talking to thin air.

Hayley looked up and nodded.

"Yes. She said you can ask the questions through me."

"That's good honey, thank you," Celeste said with a smile.

Gathering her thoughts, she grabbed her notebook and sat back down on the bed.

"Lady Louise, did you know Thaddeus Holiday?" she asked the first question to establish background information.

My memory is a bit foggy but I'll try to remember as much as I can.

Hayley repeated everything Lady Louise said.

If I recall correctly our family were friends. Yes, oh my I do remember. We would visit often during the summer.

"That's very good," Celeste responded.

"Hayley tells me you are looking for your child. Do you remember where you were the last time you saw her?"

No, that's the problem. I can't remember where she was or how I ended up here in the Manor without being able to move on.

"That's alright, we'll find the answers we're looking for, hopefully before we return home. I promise I'll do my very best to help you Lady Louise," she said.

Thank you, it is much appreciated.

"Do you remember anything at all about what happened to you or even that last day?"

It comes in bits and pieces. I do remember there was a lot of shouting. Men were arguing but that's all I remember.

Celeste wondered if there was some kind of registry or diary in the locked room in the library that could shed some light into the summers in Holiday Corner.

"If you could try to remember as much as possible. I'm going later tonight to meet up with Emily Dear who is going to help me research the history of the town in hopes that we can find something about your time here in the Manor," she said.

Thank you. I have seen her around town. She seems very nice.

"So, it's settled. Emily and I will do our very best to find out what happened to you and your daughter. And thank you Hayley, for such a great little helper. Otherwise, I wouldn't have been able to speak with Lady Louise directly," Celeste replied with a smile.

Satisfied with the way things were progressing Lady Louise left Celeste and Hayley, and she floated up to the attic and sat by the window. Focusing on the twinkling lights from Main Street she tried her very best to remember her past.

She knew she had visited Mistletoe Manor, but the rest of it came in pieces. It felt as if she was trying to put a puzzle together. The more she tried, the more jumbled the flashbacks. Taking a deep breath, she decided to head to Main Street, thinking the distraction would do her good.

Floating down to the main floor, Lady Louise looked around the living room. Children were coloring in their coloring books in the corner. A member of the staff was adding logs to the fireplace, and another had just sat down to the piano.

She left the Manor for Main Street, which was filled with both locals and tourists. Today, she would refrain from haunting them. Today, she felt better than she had felt in ages.

Back in their room, Celeste asked Hayley if she wanted to go downstairs and join the other children.

"Honey, do you want to go downstairs for a bit? According to the schedule there is a coloring table where you can choose a picture to color. When finished, those same pictures will be placed on the board by the entrance. What do you think?" she asked.

"Yes. I like to color," Hayley replied with a grin.

"Wonderful. Why don't you leave your doll here so nothing happens to her, and we can check in on her later?" Celeste asked.

"You're silly. The doll will be fine here by herself," Hayley chuckled.

Smiling Celeste extended her hand and Hayley's little fingers. Together they left their room and headed downstairs. As they approached the living area, Edwin happened to be standing nearby and asked if Hayley was there to participate in the activity.

"Welcome, Miss Hayley. Are you here to color?" he asked enthusiastically.

"Yes. I love to color," she replied with a smile.

"Well, then follow me. We have a coloring book just for you. Once you've looked through the pages you need to pick one drawing and coloring it. After it's finished, we'll hang it in the board by the entrance. How does that sound to you?"

"Alright," she answered smiling.

Before following Edwin, she looked at Celeste to make sure it was alright with her mother.

"Go on and have fun. I have to do a little work and I'll be back before you know it," she answered.

"Don't worry, you can leave Hayley with us here. She's in good hands," Edwin told Celeste.

"Thank you. I won't be long. If for any reason you need to reach me, please call me on my cell," Celeste replied.

Celeste had decided she'd visit the local newspaper to see if there were any stories about the Manor in the archives. She gathered her coat, gloves, and hat and set off in the direction of Main Street. The closer she got to the center of town, the more people she found out and about. Most waved or nodded their heads acknowledging her. She smiled each time and waved back.

As she approached the newspaper, she saw Nick Holiday walking along the street. Emily had told her he was the Mayor of Holiday Corner and a descendant of Thaddeus. She slowed her pace and when she was near enough, she called out to him.

"Mr. Mayor, may I have a word with you?"

"Of course. And who do I have the pleasure of meeting on this wonderful wintery night?"

"Oh, sorry. My name is Celeste. My daughter and I are staying at Mistletoe Manor and I'm writing an article about the history of town and the Manor. Would it be possible to ask you a few questions?"

Celeste hated to lie, but she knew telling him that she was there to investigate the town ghost would not go over very well.

"Yes, why don't we meet at the diner in about half an hour. Will that work for you?"

"That's wonderful. Yes, thank you. I have to make a stop at the newspaper and will be there shortly," she replied.

Nick was a bit curious as to why she would be going to newspaper, but quickly dismissed the thought.

Celeste entered the newspaper and was greeted by Arvin, the proprietor.

"Welcome. How may I assist you?" he asked.

"I'd like to see if you have any articles about the history of the town and specifically about Mistletoe Manor?"

"There's not a lot of information available, but I can show you what we do have, and you can decide for yourself," he stated.

"Thank you. Any information you can provide would be appreciated. By the way, is there anything in the archives about visitors who frequented Mistletoe Manor back when Thaddeus owned it?"

"Anyone in particular you are looking into?" he asked wondering what she was after.

"Yes. I'd like to know if you've ever seen anything in the archives related to a Lady Louise Rafferty," she inquired.

"No. That name doesn't sound familiar. May I ask why you're inquiring about her?"

"I believe that's the ghost that's been haunting the Manor and Holiday Corner. I also believe she frequented the Manor during the time Thaddeus owned it," she replied.

"That's a lot of information you have here Ms... um.. what is your name again?" he asked.

"I never actually introduced myself. My name is Celeste. I'm staying at Mistletoe Manor for the holidays with my daughter Hayley. Since my arrival

I've been interested in the town and the Manor. I used to visit when I was a child and had always been curious about the ghost hauntings. So, I decided to do some research," she replied.

"Very nice to meet you. Although you have piqued my interest. Why this Lady Louise Rafferty," he asked.

"It's just a name I heard around town and am trying to figure out if this indeed is the ghost everyone's been talking about," she replied, hoping he wouldn't ask any more questions.

"Well, I don't remember finding mention of a Lady Louise Rafferty, but I'll search and let you if I find anything," he said as he entered the information in the computer.

"That would be wonderful. You can either call me at the Manor or maybe someone can drop it off for me?" she inquired.

"No problem. I was planning on visiting the Manor. I'll just bring the documents to you when I'm done," he said.

"Perfect thank you," Celeste replied and left the newspaper office.

Outside, she decided to make a quick stop at the toy store to buy some last-minute gifts for Haley. She picked up clothes for the doll, a few books, and a small handmade doll bassinet. Then she waited until all of the gifts were wrapped.

Nick had just stepped outside when he noticed Celeste leaving the newspaper. He watched intently from a distance as she entered the toy store.

What was she up to and why the interest in Holiday Corner and the ghost he wondered?

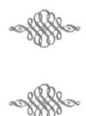

NICK ENTERED THE NEWSPAPER in search of Arvin.

"Arvin. What did that woman want?"

"No hello? How about Hi Arvin, how are you doing this cold wintery day?" he chuckled.

"Yeah, yeah. How are you and what did that woman want?"

"I'm doing well, thank you for asking," he was now messing with Nick.

"So?" He raised his hands letting him know he wanted answers.

"Fine. You are no fun. Celeste is her name. She came in here looking for information about the history of the town and Mistletoe Manor," he answered.

"Why?"

"Why not? There's a lot of history here in Holiday Corner, and she's interested in learning about our wonderful town," he replied.

"That's all?" Nick was not convinced.

He hesitated a few seconds before answering him. Then decided it couldn't hurt.

"She did ask about a Lady Louise Rafferty. She also wanted to know about the visitors that graced the Manor during the time Thaddeus owned it," he responded.

Nick didn't say anything but remained pensive. If he recalled correctly, there had been some mention of a Lady Louise Rafferty. However, he couldn't remember anything in detail. At the time, he had brushed it off as insignificant.

He worried that having some stranger interested in the ghost was troublesome. If they were interested in the history of the town, that was another thing, but the ghost? One thing was certain, he needed to make sure this so-called Lady Louise Rafferty was not the ghost that was haunting the town and the Manor now. Or at least, if that were the case, that her death had been an accident.

Most importantly, he needed to ensure the good name of Holiday was not tarnished. He would need to watch Celeste more closely. Realizing the time, he thanked Arvin and left for his meeting.

Entering the diner, he smiled and greeted everyone as he passed their tables. Seeing Celeste, his smiled widened, though it was rather strained, not quite reaching the sides of his face.

"May I sit?"

"Of course," Celeste replied.

"So, tell me how I can be of assistance?" he asked.

At that moment the waitress stopped by and he asked about her father who had been under the weather. She informed him that he was doing much better and would be back at work in a few days. He then ordered a coffee and pie. Celeste ordered the same.

"Well, as I said earlier. I'm interested in the history of the town and the Manor. When I was a child, my parents would spend the holidays here and it was such a magical place I decided I wanted to learn as much as possible," she said gauging his reaction.

"Well, from what I recall my great, great, you get the idea, Thaddeus Holiday, founded Holiday Corner back in 1892. At the time there were not a lot of people living here. He was so in love with his wife he decided to build a grand home for them, a home where they could entertain and have friends visit. He also started the tradition of the gala. Each year townspeople and friends would flock to the Manor for the festivities. It became so popular that they had to start turning people away," he said.

"That's the story my parents told me also. What a wonderful time to have lived here. I can only imagine the town and residents," she said with a smile.

"As you may know, my sister and I are descendants of Thaddeus. I'm the Mayor and very proud of that position, and my sister is in charge of all the activities and festivities in Holiday Corner. Sort of like an ambassador," he stated.

"There is one other thing I'd like to ask you," she said to him.

Taking a drink of his coffee, he looked directly at Celeste and waited.

"Can you tell me about the resident ghost?"

"I don't know anything about a ghost," he replied.

This was exactly what Nick was worried about. Here comes this stranger that starts looking into our resident ghost. Why couldn't she just leave things alone... He needed to discourage her from pursuing this line of thought.

"You know those are just rumors. There's no proof that a ghost haunts the Manor," he stated trying to sound convincing.

"What if I told you I have uncovered proof that a ghost does indeed haunt Mistletoe Manor. In fact, I even know her name. Lady Louise Rafferty. It appears she and her family frequented the Manor during the time that your ancestor lived there," she said waiting for him to debunk her theory.

"That's preposterous. I have searched endlessly and have never found anything remotely associated with a ghost or anyone with that name that visited my ancestor's home during the summers. Where are you getting this information?" He sounded agitated.

"I'd rather keep my source out of this for now," she replied.

"Well, you need to be careful spreading such rumors around town. Townspeople will not take kindly to false statements, especially if they have to do with Thaddeus," he responded.

"Oh, no. I would never spread rumors. As I mentioned, I'm just trying to figure out who the ghost is while learning the history of the town and, of course, the Manor," she replied with a smile.

Celeste realized she needed to tread carefully around Nick Holiday. It was obvious he didn't want any negative stories affecting his beloved Holiday Corner. There was no way he'd cooperate by providing any information, or making even any of the documents he had available. She'd just have to rely on Emily's help and that of Lady Louise herself. Wanting to liven up the mood, she inquired as to the family home.

"Actually, tell me about the Manor. It's such a beautiful home," she said with a smile.

"Aww, yes, it's a magnificent building. Thaddeus built the house for his wife. During the time he lived in the house, they entertained often whenever they were in town. Later, when Thaddeus and his family passed away it was passed down from generation to generation. My father unfortunately had no interest in the house and it sat for many years untouched. That is, until Edwin Bowater arrived in town," he said stopping to take a bite of his pie.

"The structure of the building is indeed magnificent," she replied.

"Since buying the Manor, Edwin has done a wonderful job of restoring it to its glory years. It looks almost as it did back when Thaddeus first built it. He even has brought back the gala every year. This is one event I look forward to, even the townspeople get into the spirit of the festivities surrounding the event," he smiled, happy the conversation was moving in another direction.

"Did you ever live in the Manor?"

"No, but I visited often when my grandparents owned it. I would run around and get lost in the Manor, especially down in the cellar where they keep all of the liquor." He laughed at the memory. Those were good times.

"Oh, I can only imagine the games you must have played there," Celeste smiled warmly.

"Well, I'm sorry but that's all the time I have. If there are any other questions, don't hesitate to reach out. I'm certain I'll be seeing you around town and possibly at the gala?"

"I quite understand. Yes, you'll see me around town as I want to show Hayley, my daughter, as much of Holiday Corner as possible. And of course, I'll be attending the gala," she replied with a smile.

Standing up she extended her arm to shake his hand. His grip was stronger than she'd expected, but she thought nothing of it.

After paying her bill, she exited the diner and headed back to the Manor. There were several questions that she needed answering and she hoped Lady Louise would be available to speak with her.

BACK AT THE NEWSPAPER, Arvin thought about Celeste's visit. He decided there may be some validity to her inquires. So, he focused his research on finding out as much as possible about this Lady Louise. The more he searched the more he realized there was indeed information about parties and events at Thaddeus' home that might be also useful for the article he wanted to write.

Digging through article after article, Arvin finally found what he'd been looking for in the society section. There was a story about a prominent family, Lord and Lady Rafferty visiting for the first time. It mentioned a Lady Louise, her husband, and her child. The article went on to say how thrilled they were to be able to visit and spend some time with their friends during the hot summer season. Another article talked about how Lord and Lady Rafferty would spend the winter holiday at the Manor while Thaddeus and his family traveled to other parts of the country.

He continued to search and luckily found additional articles related to activities around Holiday Corner in which Lady Louise and her family were mentioned. Then it suddenly stopped, there was no more mention of the family, or in fact any stories about the activities or even the gala. The next articles he found were rather disturbing. The first article mentioned an incident at the Manor that left several people dead including Thaddeus and his family. It was not specific, however, as to whom was in the house and what had actually happened.

He found another article that detailed those killed as members of the Sinclair family, and the Rafferty family. The article later clarified that only Lord Rafferty was found dead. Lady Louise and her daughter were not found among the bodies. They speculated that Lady Louise and her child were able to escape, though they were never heard from again.

Incredible that he never knew this information existed. Could this Lady Louise Rafferty actually be the ghost that haunted the Manor? Could she have met with her demise and never escaped as many believed? He wondered.

While Arvin was compiling the information he had gathered, Nick was stewing about the new developments concerning Celeste. He wasn't happy with the fact that she was digging into the history of the Manor. It was the same reason that he hadn't satisfied Edwin's request. This Celeste person was doing exactly what he had tried so desperately to avoid.

Celeste returned to the Manor and went directly to her room to hide the gifts she purchased for Hayley. In the quiet of her room, she sat and jotted notes of everything she had learned today, as well as, her thoughts about her meeting at the local newspaper and with the mayor.

When she was finished, she went in search of Hayley. She found Haylee talking with some of the other children and giggling. It pleased her to see her daughter so happy. As she watched, it didn't seem as if Lady Louise was anywhere in site, or least, she wasn't talking to Hayley.

Deciding to wait a bit, Celeste went to the library in search of a book about the town, and was soon settled by the fire, having lost track of time.

When Hayley walked-up and stood beside her, Celeste jumped.

"Oh no, did I scare you mommy?" she asked with a twinkle in her eyes.

"Yes, you did indeed," Celeste laughed.

Hayley was excited to tell her about everything she did from the moment she'd picked out her coloring book. By the time she finished her story Celeste was laughing.

"Well, well. It seems you had an amazing time honey. I'm so very glad you've made some new friends and are enjoying yourself," she said with a smile.

"Yes, I did, mommy."

"By the way, have you spoken with Lady Louise today?" she inquired.

"No. She hasn't stopped by for visit," Hayley replied.

"Do you think if we go upstairs you can try to reach her? There are a few questions I have that I'd like to ask her if that's possible?"

"I don't know mommy. We can try," she replied as she shrugged her shoulders.

"Wonderful. Are you ready to head up there now?"

"Yes, good idea mommy. I need to check in on my doll," she said rather seriously.

Smiling, Celeste kissed her and hugged her tightly, then together they went up to their room.

Once they were settled, Celeste asked her to see if Lady Louise was around or if she could summon her.

"Hello? Lady Louise, are you around? Hello?" Hayley called out.

The air suddenly shifted and Celeste knew immediately that Lady Louise was there in the room with them.

Yes, my dear I'm here. How are you doing?

"I'm well thank you," Hayley replied, and waited for Celeste to ask her questions.

"Lady Louise, I wanted to first let you know that I stopped by the newspaper and spoke with Arvin the proprietor. He's researching the archives for any mention of you or your family and said he'd bring any articles he finds over to the Manor sometime today," she said.

Tell her I'm extremely grateful. There are a few more things I've started to remember that might be helpful.

"Before you tell me what you've remembered, I wanted to also let you know that I had a meeting with the Mayor, Nick Holiday. He is a direct descendant of Thaddeus, the founder of Holiday Corner. I believe you may have known him from those times you said you visited," she said.

Yes, I do remember Thaddeus. That's one of the things I'm starting to put together. Our families were very close. I was good friends with his wife and my husband was a business partner with Thaddeus on some of his ventures. We would spend summers together here in town. But we also would visit during the holiday seasons.

"Now we're getting somewhere. Anything else you can remember?"

I do remember one day late in the evening I heard men shouting. It sounded as if it was coming from the foyer. As I stepped out to investigate, I saw one of the maids running and crying. I couldn't understand what was happening and then I'm sorry to say I remember nothing more. I can't remember when this happened or why she was crying or who was doing all the shouting. I'm sorry.

"That a lot and extremely helpful. Every little bit you can remember is essential in putting together the whole story of how you came to be a ghost. I believe your remains are still here in the Manor. We just have to find out what happened, then hopefully, we can give you a proper burial," Celeste said warmly. Then she asked a rather delicate question.

"I'm sorry and I hope you're not offended, but I must ask. Did you have an affair with Thaddeus?" she asked in almost a whisper.

Such insolence. How dare you ask such a horrid question?

The air in the room became even colder and Celeste braced herself.

"As I said, I'm sorry I have to ask, but there have been some rumors in the past that you were having an affair with Thaddeus. They believe someone killed you to keep you quiet. Now, I have spoken to Emily Dear and she doesn't believe the rumor. She says most of the townspeople don't either. Everyone here believes that Thaddeus was madly in love with his wife. I just had to ask, I'm sorry," Celeste said.

Fine. I'll accept your apology because I can tell you are genuinely trying to figure out what happened to me and help me find my daughter. So, to answer your question I don't believe I was having an affair with Thaddeus. That would have been something I would have remembered. I loved my husband very much and especially my daughter and I would never have done something as terrible as that.

"That's what I thought also. Good. Alright so, try to keep remembering as much as you can. In the interim, I'm meeting Emily tonight in the library. She has informed me that there's a secret room where all of the documents pertaining to Holiday Corner and Thaddeus are kept. I'm hoping we can find more information there to help with our quest," she stated with a smile.

Thank you. I'll let you know if I remember anything else and while you're gone, I'll watch over Hayley.

After dinner, Edwin had organized a reading. An elderly woman dressed as Mrs. Santa sat by the fireplace reading Christmas stories.

Hayley went and sat by her new friends as Celeste approached Edwin.

"Edwin, I need to step out for a little while. Can you possibly watch over Hayley?" she inquired.

"Of course. Your daughter will be busy for at least an hour. Will that be enough time?" he asked.

"Yes, thank you very much," Celeste replied.

She kissed Hayley, told her to behave, and that she'd be back soon. She then gathered her coat, gloves, and hat and made her way to the library.

53

WHEN CELESTE ARRIVED at the library, she noticed Emily at the side of the building. She waved, urging her to come to the back of the building.

"Good evening. Let's do this quickly as I don't want anyone to notice us lurking around the library," Emily said as she retrieved her keys.

Opening the back entrance, she gestured for Celeste to enter first and then Emily followed and shut the door behind her.

"Follow me," she instructed Celeste.

They walked in silence until they reached the third floor, and went to the back of the room. There was a panel in the wall that, unless you were looking specifically for it, you wouldn't notice. The panel had a very small key hole.

Emily walked right up to it and inserted a tiny key that had been attached to her key ring. She entered and turned on the overhead light. Celeste followed her inside and saw there was a leather couch, with a table and a lamp on each end. One wall was filled with books, the other opposite wall had two filing cabinets, and the third wall had a glass cabinet with something inside. She couldn't quite make out from where she was standing.

Moving closer into the room she spotted the cabinet. Inside was what appeared to be some kind of diary. Upon closer inspection it seemed it may have belonged to Thaddeus's wife. As it said something about the garden and the birds chirping above the trees.

Turning around, she noticed Emily had one of the filing cabinets open and had taken out several files and was placing them on the table in the center of the room. She then went to the wall with the books and retrieved a large book, also placing it on the table. For now, Emily left the diary where it was safely secured in the glass cabinet.

"Alright. I believe these might have what we're looking for. You take the book; I'll review the files. Be careful how you handle these as they are very delicate," she told Celeste.

For the next hour, they worked in silence. Every once in a while, one would exclaim with hock or a sigh. Until finally Celeste closed the book and looked at Emily. Finally, Emily stood and walked over the cabinet and retrieved the diary. She placed it on the desk next to Celeste.

"This once belonged to Thaddeus's wife. It is not to ever leave this room and you are not to speak of it to anyone. This is for your eyes only," Emily said as she walked back to her seat.

Celeste spent the next hour reading through the diary, every once in a while, looking up at Emily. Emily in turn would nod and smile. When Celeste had finished reading the diary, she closed the book and took a deep breath before speaking.

"Emily. I believe I have found enough evidence to prove that Lady Louise Rafferty did indeed frequent the Thaddeus home. They were all friends and there's no indication of there ever being an affair. As a matter of fact, they were very good friends," she smiled.

"That's wonderful news. I'm glad to put that rumor to rest. I found receipts of food and other things they ordered for specific festivities they had during that time. I also found instructions for the staff on who stayed in what room and what they needed before their arrival. I have found specific instructions for the Rafferty family," she also smiled at her findings.

"Tell me about what you found," Celeste said.

"One document instructs the staff that they need to make sure the room is ready for Lord and Lady Louise Rafferty and their child. They ordered a crib be brought to the room next door and a nanny to be brought in during their stay to watch over the child. There were several insignificant instructions on an activity, or an event happening on the grounds that concerned the Rafferty family, and even mention of one of the galas where they needed to ensure a gown was ready for Lady Louise as they were celebrating her birthday," Emily said with a smile.

"I just can't believe no one ever thought of looking to see if the ghost was someone who frequented the Manor. Instead, they just ignored it, ignored her. So sad," Celeste commented.

"My dear, some people prefer to just ignore things."

"Now that you mention it, I met with Mayor Holiday earlier and found his answers rather evasive. I felt as if he was trying to sway me away from investigating anything to do with the ghost, which I found rather peculiar," she informed her.

"He's the kind of man that doesn't want anything to tarnish the family name. Any indication that there may be some truth to the rumors or that someone may have died in the Manor, is just something he's not willing to accept," Emily said as she shrugged her shoulders.

"I think you're absolutely correct."

"We need to head out. We've been here for close to two hours and I don't want us to get caught. Let's put everything away and rendezvous back at the Manor. You leave first and make sure no one sees you leaving, and after I lock up, I'll come meet you at Mistletoe Manor," Emily instructed her.

Celeste nodded, gathered everything she had been reviewing, and replaced them where they had been found. She then thanked Emily again and headed out the door.

Little did she know that Nick happened to be walking by and noticed her walking out from behind the library. That confirmed his suspicion that Celeste was digging into things and snooping around where she wasn't welcome. He needed to put a stop to this before something awful happened.

Nick moved into the shadows so that he was not seen. Celeste walked quickly back in the direction of Mistletoe Manor. As Nick was about to walk away, he noticed Emily Dear walking out of the library.

Not only is Arvin researching information for Celeste, but so is Emily. I need to put a stop this, he thought to himself.

He took out his phone and dialed his sister.

"Joy, we have a problem," he said into the receiver.

"What's going on?" she asked rather alarmed.

"It seems there's a guest staying at the Mistletoe Manor, a Celeste that has been asking around town about Holiday Corner and our resident ghost. She's even gone to see Arvin and now I see that Emily Dear is also helping her find answers," he stated rather annoyed.

"Are you kidding me? What's wrong with you? There's nothing wrong with someone taking an interest in our history. Is there something you're not telling me?"

"Not specifically. I'm just afraid that if they dig up some dirt, it'll damage our family, our family name," he stated rather sternly.

"Oh please, are you serious? Even if that were true, so what? Our townspeople don't care. They love us so much it doesn't matter. Stop worrying, I'm too busy to be dealing with this right now," she replied and hung up the phone.

Fine, I'll just have to handle this myself, he thought.

GHOSTLY GIFT

BACK AT THE MANOR, Celeste found Hayley fast asleep in one of the chairs by the fireplace. Most of the children had fallen asleep. Edwin had provided warm milk and cookies and that had done the trick.

Celeste smiled as she approached. Behind her Edwin whispered.

"They're all fast asleep. They cuddled up close to each other and one by one closed their eyes and here they are," he chuckled.

"That must have been quite a story," Celeste chuckled.

Edwin nodded asking her if she'd gotten everything she needed done.

"Yes, thank you. I was actually searching for information, any information I could gather on Holiday Corner and Mistletoe Manor. I'm looking specifically for information related to someone who I believe frequented the Manor during the time that Thaddeus lived here with his family. I've been able to uncover the name Lady Louise Rafferty. It seems she may be the ghost that haunts the town and more importantly, the Manor," she said.

"No kidding? I've asked Nick, the mayor to find information for me and he has informed me there was nothing available, especially having to do with a ghost." He seemed rather pensive.

"Well, I've uncovered that Lady Louise frequented the Manor during the summers with her husband and child, and sometimes during the holiday season. I can tell you it appears that she is the ghost that haunts the town. I've confirmed that the rumor of her having an affair with Thaddeus was just fabrication. There is no basis to that story. In addition, I can tell you that there was mention of her and her family in several articles until they suddenly stopped completely. After that the only thing I could find was an argument that apparently erupted here in the Manor, and that several people died seemingly as a result. It is also believed that her husband died and that she and her child escaped. Except we know that if she's the ghost haunting Holiday Corner and the Manor, then she didn't escape. That means her remains and possibly those of her child are buried somewhere in the Manor."

"Wow. I can't believe you found this information. That's more than I've been able to uncover during the time that I've searched," he replied.

Shortly after, Arvin arrived with a handful of papers. He approached Celeste who had been sitting with some of the guests discussing upcoming activities.

"Excuse me, Celeste. May I have a word with you?" Arvin asked.

"Yes, of course. If you all will excuse me," she said as she stood and walked toward Arvin.

"This is everything I have been able to find. Lady Louise Rafferty did exist and she did visit with her family often," he said.

"Thank you. I'm aware of that, did you find anything else?" she asked.

"Several articles talked about events around town and the Manor. One in particular was about an argument that erupted where several people were killed. One staff member was quoted as saying it was pandemonium. She said she remembered Lady Louise Rafferty running into her bedroom and closing the door and then her husband running with the child down to the cellar. After that there's not much else written. The next article talked about how everything changed after that incident," he stated.

"This is very helpful."

Just then, Nick walked in and glanced around the room. He settled his eyes on them as they were talking. As he approached them, he heard Arvin saying he'd continue looking for anything else about the Rafferty family and would let her know.

"Hello. How's everyone doing?" Nick asked.

They each responded that everything was good. Arvin informed Nick that he had found some interesting information about a Lady Louise Rafferty, but quickly stated there was nothing scandalous. That pleased Nick.

After he heard that, he felt much better about Celeste's inquiries. Their conversation moved on to the upcoming gala and other activities around town.

Shortly afterward, Nick excused himself from the group. He mentioned a phone call he needed to make, and left the Manor. Arvin followed. During this time Emily had noticed them talking and gone into the kitchen undetected. She wanted to stay out of the way until everyone had gone. When she was certain Arvin and Nick had left, she returned to the living area where Celeste was gathering Hayley.

"Oh, here you are. I'm heading upstairs to see if Lady Louise will speak with me now that I have much more information. Would you like to join us?"

"Yes. That would be wonderful," she replied and followed Celeste up to their room.

Once they were settled in the room Hayley called out to Lady Louise. They could tell when she appeared as the temperature changed immediately.

"Good evening, Lady Louise. This is Emily Dear who has been instrumental in helping me learn more about you, and your family, and your visits to the Manor," Celeste said.

She repeated everything she had learned, including the articles she had read. As Celeste spoke, Lady Louise began to remember what had happened that dreadful day. Taking a deep breath, she recalled the events.

I remember hearing voices. Someone was shouting that they would kill me and my child if my husband didn't agree to their demands. They also threatened Thaddeus and his family who had just recently returned to the Manor. Thaddeus and my husband demanded the intruders leave immediately to no avail. At that moment, I left the library where I'd been reading a book, to find my husband running towards me. He told me to hide in the secret room he had shown me a while back and that he would bring our child to me.

She paused for a moment lost in thought before she continued.

It's all coming back to me. My husband must have been killed because he never returned for me. When I finally was able to leave the hidden space, I was no longer part of the living. I searched and searched the Manor and couldn't find anyone.

"Lady Louise, I may know where your child is. It seems that I was able to find an article where a maid remembered seeing your husband run down to the cellar with your child. Maybe he couldn't reach you and thought that might be the best place to hide," Celeste informed her.

The cellar? It never occurred to me to even consider the Manor's cellar.

And with that she disappeared. A few seconds later she returned.

I have found my daughter; my poor child has been here all this time.

Hayley could see the child standing next to Lady Louise.

"Hi," she said.

Celeste and Emily looked at Hayley rather confused.

"Mommy, Lady Louise found her daughter. She's standing right here with her. You were right, she was in the cellar," Hayley said with a smile.

"Oh my, that's wonderful news," Emily stated as she clapped her hands.

"Indeed," Celeste agreed with a huge grin.

"We'll look for your daughter's remains, but for now we need to find the hidden crawl space. Do you think you can show us?" Celeste asked.

Yes, it's actually here in this room. You'll need to move that dresser. Behind there is a small opening hardly visible. Pushing the wall right in the middle of the square should cause it to open.

Hayley made sure Celeste pushed exactly where Lady Louise indicated, and the section of wall popped opened.

Celeste and Emily looked at each other in shock. Celeste, being quite agile, got on her knees and crawled into the space. When she gasped everyone knew she'd found Lady Louise's remains.

Immediately, Emily went in search of Edwin. who in turn called Frank. The next few hours the Manor were filled with people. When everyone had finally gone and the remains of Lady Louise and her child had been removed, Celeste, Hayley, Edwin, Emily, Arvin, Nick and Joy gathered around the fireplace.

"I can't believe she was real and here all of these years," Edwin stated.

"It's incredible that such an injustice happened so long ago to the Holiday and Rafferty family," Edwin stated with a sigh.

Over the next few days, everyone talked about what had happened so many years ago.

On the night of the gala, all of the townspeople showed up. The celebration focused around both families, honoring them and the sacrifices they had made, and the inability of the local police force in not finding the bodies of Lady Louise and her child. They learned however, that Lady Louise's husband was found in the foyer of the Manor never having had an opportunity to tell anyone where his wife and daughter were hiding.

During the gala, Lady Louise and her daughter made one last appearance. Speaking for Lady Louise, Hayley told everyone that she was very grateful for everything that had been done, and for finally helping to reunite her with her family. For a brief moment Lady Louise, her husband, and daughter appeared, to the surprise of everyone present and just like that disappeared to never haunt again.

The next day, on the front page of the Holiday Times in bold letters, was the story everyone was talking about; *Lady Louise Rafferty and Daughter Found at Last.*

Celeste sat in the corner of the living area reading the article. As promised, this was one holiday Celeste and the rest of the town would never forget.

THE END

Author's Note

This three-book series was so much fun to write! We are hoping to continue with more stories next year.

For now, make sure to pick up a copy of all three books. Paperbacks are also available.

Book 1 – Missing Santas by Sharon Michaels

Book 2 – Ghostly Gift by Ileana Muñoz Renfroe

Book 3 – Slay Ride by Donna B McNicol.

LIST OF PUBLISHED AND UPCOMING WORK

COZY MYSTERY BOOKS:
Rosa The Cuban Psychic Paranormal Cozy Mysteries

- Book 1: A Fashionable Fate
- Book 2: A Parisian Bait
- Raul's Demise (Prequel)
- Book 3: A Mysterious Date

Wisterious Bay Cozy Paranormal Mysteries

- Book 1: The Wisterious Witch
- Book 2: The Banished Reaper
- Book 3: A Humorous Skeleton

A Tarot and Vintage Caravan Cuban Cozy Mystery Series

- Murder at The Campground

A Candeedo Brewdinkle Mystery Series

- Cipher, Mobsters & A Sphynx

Lolita Restoration Cozy Mystery Series

- If Walls Could Talk

Mrs. Greneerie Cozy Mystery Series

+ Aunt Greneerie and The Missing Pocket Watch

The Shoemaker Mystery Series

• The Hidden Secret

CHILDREN'S BOOK:
Gizmo Adventures

+ Gizmo Welcomes A New Baby
+ Gizmo and Ellie's First Outing

NOTEBOOKS:

+ My Holiday Corner Notebook
• My Notes - Las Cubanitas Journal
• My Notes - Cat Journal
• My Notes - Raul Journal
• My Notes - Candeedo Brewdinkle Journal
• My Notes - Abuela Nana from A Tarot and Vintage Caravan Journal
• My Notes - Dog Journal
• My Notes - Quirky Characters
• My Notes - Gizmo and Family Journal
• My Notes - Golf Journal
• My Notes - Rosa de Los Reyes Journal
• My Tarot Journal
• My Anxiety Journal
• My Aura Journal
• My Bird Watching Journal
• My Daily Journal

- My Notes Recipe Journal
- My Notes - Favorite Restaurants

Did you enjoy this book?

•

*I*f you enjoyed reading Ghostly Gift or any of my other books, please consider leaving a review.

•

Amazon.com: Ileana Munoz Renfroe: Books, Biography, Blog, Audiobooks, Kindle[1]

About the Author

AUTHOR BIO

For the longest time, Ileana Muñoz-Renfroe wanted to be an author. Almost twenty years later, and after raising two children and owning numerous businesses, she decided to take the plunge.

Ileana was born in Cuba and raised in New York City's Washington Heights neighborhood. Yes, in The Heights, just as Lin-Manuel Miranda portrayed it—complete with abuelas spying over the neighborhood from their windowsill, Bodega owners welcoming you by name and chasing off graffiti artists, and everyone being involved in everyone's business. A large family who would gather every evening downstairs to watch the children play as the adults gossiped. It was welcoming and cozy.

In 2020, as Ileana sat in a Café in Paris, the idea of Rosa popped into her head, and the stories and characters became real. Since two of her passions are the paranormal and high-end fashion, she found a way to combine them by creating Rosa The Cuban Psychic Mysteries. This series brings together her Cuban and American culture to make for a fun cozy mystery story. This is her debut novel.

She is hard at work on writing book 3 of The Cuban Psychic Mystery Series. In this book, Rosa de Los Reyes has returned to Colten Island hoping to relax only to find trouble in every turn.

In addition, she's released Raul's Demise, a prequel to Rosa The Cuban Psychic Cozy Mysteries.

She has published TWO new series. One, is The Wisterious Witch (Wisterious Bay Cozy Paranormal Mystery, book 1), AND Ghostly Gift (Holiday Corner Christmas Cozy Mystery, book 2).

The new series, A Tarot and Caravan Mystery Series will be out this year with surprise adventures featuring Abuela Nana.

In addition to that, she is almost done with another new series - Candeedo Brewdinkle the nosy detective who loves to decipher codes. As a retired spy he is thrust back into action when bodies start piling up all around him.

GHOSTLY GIFT

The new children's book - Gizmo Welcomes A New Baby has been a huge success. Look for more books upcoming in the series - Gizmo Adventures.

When she is not writing, she enjoys spending time with family and friends, travelling, reading, entertaining, and listening to music.

To ensure you are kept informed of the latest news, join me in the various social media platforms.

Don't forget to sign up for the newsletter and the birthday club.

<u>Newsletter and Birthday Club</u>[1]
<u>Instagram</u>[2]
<u>Twitter</u>[3]
<u>Facebook Author Page</u> [4]
<u>Facebook - Cozy Mystery Village</u>[5]
<u>Facebook – Renfroe's Reading Room</u>[6]
<u>Twisty Tales and Cozy Crimes</u>[7]
<u>Holiday Corner Christmas Cozies</u>[8]

---

1. *https://www.imrenfroe.com/newsletter*

2. *https://www.instagram.com/imrenfroe/*

3. *https://twitter.com/IleanaRenfroe*

4. *https://www.facebook.com/imrenfroe*

5. *https://www.facebook.com/groups/cozymysteryvillage/*

6. *https://www.facebook.com/groups/renfroesreadingroom*

7. *https://www.facebook.com/
    twistytalesandcozycrimes/?show_switched_toast=0&show_invite_to_follow=0&show_sw
    itched_tooltip=0&show_podcast_settings=0&show_community_transition=0&show_co
    mmunity_review_changes=0&show_community_rollback=0&show_follower_visibility_
    disclosure=0*

8. *https://www.facebook.com/groups/holidaycorner*

The Holiday Corner Christmas Cozy Mystery Series

Book 1 – Missing Santas

Event planner Joy Holiday isn't exactly feeling joyful this Christmas season. Joy's job has quickly turned into saving the town's holiday season and putting an end to the chaos.

Holiday Corner, Vermont, is a close-knit mountain town that prides itself on showing it's Christmas spirit 365 days a year. For some reason, this year's Christmas celebration seems to be plagued by misfortune and mayhem. Someone is out to ruin the festivities and lay the blame on Joy Holiday.

Who dislikes Joy so much that they are willing to commit murder?

Book 2 – Ghostly Gift

Now with the Manor restored and the traditional gala preparations underway, Edwin does not have time for Lady Louise Rafferty. She roams the Manor and the town scaring the guests and visitors.

Celeste and her daughter Hayley, arrive for a week's stay just in time for the festivities. What Celeste didn't expect is that before long she, along with the town's grandmotherly figure, would be solving the mystery of the haunting ghost.

Who killed Lady Louise Rafferty and why hasn't anyone found her body? And why is she insisting on finding her daughter?

Book 3 – Slay Ride

Cany Cane Carriages – a sweet place to die

It's a celebration year-round in Holiday Corner, a scenic small town tucked away in Vermont. Candy canes, garlands, ornaments, wreaths and more – who would expect to find a dead body?

Certainly not the owners of Candy Cane Carriages, provider of winter sleigh rides. Nor their twin granddaughters, Candi and Mandi Winter who have come to help them run the business.

But when Gavin Foster, a local photographer and animal rights activist is found dead in one of their sleights, they find one of them will be accused of his murder.

ALL THREE ARE AVAILABLE ON AMAZON

https://www.amazon.com/gp/product/B0BLHGR1PV

RECIPE

CREMA DE VIE/EGGNOG

Ingredients

Simple syrup

1 cup granulated white sugar

1 cup water

Crema de Vie

1 can sweetened condensed milk

1 can evaporated milk

6 egg yolks from pasteurized eggs

1 cup dark rum

1 tsp Pure vanilla extract not artificial

Cinnamon, ground, and/or sticks for garnish

Instructions

Simple syrup

Over medium-low heat put equal parts of water and white sugar into a saucepan and stir. Once the sugar has dissolved into the water remove it from the heat and let it cool.

Crema de Vie Cocktail

In a blender, gently mix eggs. Add evaporated milk and condensed milk and gently blend until smooth.

Can be made without the Rum and it's still yummy. Enjoy!